I0688700

AFTERMATH

The Vaedra Chronicles Series Book 4

ESTER LÓPEZ

WPS

Writing & Photographic Services LLC

ESTER'S READERS GROUP

Copyright © 2020 by Ester López

Writing & Photographic Services LLC

All characters in this book are fictitious and any resemblance to actual persons living or dead, places, events, or locales is purely coincidental.

All rights reserved.

No part of this book may be reproduced in any form or by any electronic or mechanical means, including information storage and retrieval systems, without written permission from the author, except for the use of brief quotations in a book review.
Please do not participate in or encourage piracy of copyrighted materials in violation of the author's rights. All characters and storylines are the property of the author and your support and respect is appreciated.
This book contains mature content and is intended for adult readers.
Cover design by ebooklaunch.com
ISBN: 978-1-7347536-7-7
eBook ISBN: 978-1-7347536-8-4

*For all those in our military who fight to keep our nation safe
and for all those in the Space Force
who fight to keep the planet safe,
thanks for your service and may
God be with you!*

❦   I   ❦

Atlantic Ocean, Off the Coast of Florida

"I got a big one, Dad!"

"Fight it, Jimmy. Don't lose it. Eddie, get the gaff hook."

Eddie moved behind his brother to grab the gaff. A strange light, moving rapidly underwater toward their boat, caught his attention. What would be out here late at night? Eddie pulled out his phone and started filming it.

Dave moved behind Jimmy to help him hold onto the pole. "Eddie! Where's that gaff hook?"

"Dad! Look at this!" Eddie shouted.

Dave glanced toward Eddie. The ocean lit up around the boat. Dave was thrown off balance as Jimmy fell into his arms. One hand was around his son, the other held the pole. Dave swung his attention to the bow of the boat as it lifted out of the water. He and Jimmy fell back against the cabin. The giant grouper fell on top of Jimmy, thrashing and kicking. Before them, a space ship wider than six cabin cruisers lifted out of the water with two more ships on each side of it.

Their boat slammed back into the water.

"Eddie? Are you all right?"

"I got it, Dad! I got it on my phone."

Before he could show his dad the film, more lights came toward them from under the ocean.

Eddie turned around and filmed it. This time, the space ships did not lift the boat, but came out farther ahead of them in the water. These five ships were about the same size as the first five.

"Call the Coast Guard, Dad," Jimmy said.

"Who is going to believe it, son?"

Eddie took a picture of Jimmy with his fish. "I sent it to the local news. They'll believe the film footage, Dad. This is news!"

Altay Mountains, Russia

A group of hikers on an outing looked up at the mountains and saw six UFOs fly out from the mountain range and head up into space. One of the hikers pulled out his camera and took pictures of the ships before they disappeared.

Virginia Countryside

Mr. and Mrs. McGuire sat in their living room and watched the news reports about the alien exodus.

"I think we should go and stay at Keely's apartment in D.C.," Mrs. McGuire said.

"Why? We've had the implants taken out."

"Yes, but they may still find us. They know where we live."

Mr. McGuire stood up. "You're right, honey. We better start packing."

Situation Room, White House, Washington, DC

"The latest reports from around the world shows a mass exodus of space ships heading into space. Here are some images from Russia. Then we have some from the Pacific

Ocean and the Mediterranean Sea. The last is a video from the coast of Florida."

The President and his key officials watched the screen as a newscaster reported. The president sat forward in his seat. "Has General Yermolay decided to talk?"

"He's talking to his lawyer, sir," his aide replied.

"This secret government stops now. This thing Truman started has snowballed into a giant mess. Now we have these aliens, living on our planet, secretly working with a select few for the benefit of that select few. I want answers and I want them now. If we have to arrest everyone involved to get answers, then so be it. The future of this planet is at stake and it all falls back on this secret government."

"I believe the DOJ have arrested about forty people so far, sir."

"Someone needs to start talking. The aliens are planning something and it doesn't look good."

~

Space, The Concordance

Captain Gadara ni Hovsep sat at her Nav-U-Comm, watching the six pilots take turns landing their class A wing ships, otherwise known as military escorts, into the Concordance's landing bays.

"Easy and steady. There you go. Good job! Next!"

She could see the four remaining pilots holding behind the Concordance, waiting their turns.

She had already taught them how to fly the wedges and these military escort ships. All that was left were the transporters. When this group finished their tour with the Concordance, she would finally get her promotion to Mission Specialist and be in the next Exploration Group, leaving the

Vaedra System. She had done everything she set out to do with the military. Anything higher than Captain in the military meant more paperwork and she refused to do any more of that. Now, she wanted more action.

She wanted to see what else was out there. The Earth system seemed interesting enough, but that planet was well populated. Did they even explore their own system? Were there people on the other planets rotating around their sun?

She didn't get her questions answered because she had been training these six new pilots for the Vaedran Military. While Admiral Esrith had the Concordance hovering over Earth, waiting for his mission to end, she had her own mission.

These pilots seemed ready. They took all the sim training and manual training she gave them. This last part was actual flight training maneuvers, most of it spent flying around Earth and its moon. Every scenario she could think of, she threw at them, and they handled it well. They tried landings on Earth's oceans and on the moon's surface. It was tense for a while when they lost communications on the moon. And being fired at by those lunar people gave her pilots some live escape practice. Were those lunar people the same people who lived on Earth? Why did they shoot at them? They were just practicing landings on rough surfaces. If their communications hadn't been jammed, the lunar people would have known that.

She was anxious to talk to Eno and find out how the Earth pilots did with their brief training. Were they difficult to work with? Were they fast learners? After his rescue, he took some of the best Vaedran pilots to Earth to train their best pilots.

There was one more flight scheduled for her trainees, but that would be after they made the jump. It would be landing at the Timucan Space Station between Vestra Major and

Persus. They had already practiced space jumps, so she was looking forward to the landing. Space station landings could be tricky. Once they passed this test, the rest was all about flight time. If they wanted promotions, they needed to fly more.

Now, she looked forward to some time off. And a tall drink. It was her turn to land. She pulled into the hanger as the Concordance closed up the landing ramp. She waited for pressurization before opening her door.

The rest of her crew gathered around her ship, waiting for orders.

"Okay guys, you're off the next two days. Report to our Sim Room at 0900 hours on Monday."

"Yes!" A couple shouted from the group.

"And don't be late!" She couldn't get out of there fast enough. She still had to write up the reports on each man and how they performed for this part of their training. But that could wait. Drink first, paperwork later.

Gadara headed to the Officers Lounge on deck 1. She checked her chrono. It was early. She wouldn't have to put up with anyone at this hour. Most officers showed up after the evening meal.

She took the stairs. The people movers were too slow for her. She had energy to burn and this would help. By the time she got to deck 1, she saw Admiral Esrith walk into the lounge ahead of her.

Damn! She wanted to drink alone. Esrith liked to talk. She moved to the bar on the side away from the admiral.

"Hello, Captain!" Lieutenant Eno ni Esrith said. Eno was taller than his 6'5" admiral father, but with his white-blond hair and pale blue eyes, was otherwise the spitting image of his Chromian parent. Both men were pleasant to look at, but could be very intimidating when they wanted to be.

"Lieutenant," she nodded. "I'll have a Detonator," she said to the barkeep. It was the strongest drink she could tolerate.

"Something must be going on to have three officers in here this early," Lieutenant Eno said as he sipped his drink.

"Something indeed," Admiral Esrith said, moving toward them.

"I'll say," the barkeep added. "This is the fifth Detonator I've made in the last ten minutes.

Gadara glanced at the two Esrith men and the barkeep. "Who are the other two for?"

Before he could answer, the door hissed open and two people stepped inside.

"Lieutenant Tremol and Keely." Admiral Esrith raised his glass to them. "I believe you know Lieutenant Tremol, Captain Gadara?"

"Lieutenant Tremol of the Interplanetary Space Patrol?" she asked. Tremol was definitely Caucus with his dark hair and brown eyes, but he had two inches on her six-foot frame. She'd seen him on the ship before arriving in Earth's atmosphere.

"Yes, and this is his mate, Keely ni Tremol, a Secret Service Agent from the Earthen Delegation. They recently met on Earth and I performed the ceremony here on the Concordance."

Keely was definitely new. She would have remembered someone like her with all that dark orange hair, blue eyes, and all those little brown dots across her face.

"She looks like the Huanti from Plexus," Gadara said.

"That's what Tremol told me when we first met," Keely said. "I know this was a short engagement period. We barely know each other, but I feel as if we get along well, we're both in law enforcement, and we have a lifetime to get to know each other." She glanced at Tremol and smiled.

"They are the first liaisons for the new Delegations between Earth and Vaedra," Lieutenant Eno added.

The barkeep slid two Detonators toward Tremol and one toward Gadara.

Tremol reached for the two drinks and handed one to Keely. Gadara picked up her Detonator.

"May we get to our destination unencumbered." The admiral toasted them.

The five officers lifted their glasses and sipped their drinks when the door to the Officers Lounge hissed open.

❦   2   ❦

All five people and the barkeep turned toward the man standing in the doorway.

Keely realized that all the officers wore white flight suits with different insignias and colored bars over their left breast. This man appeared to be a lower rank, in a white uniform with no insignia.

"Admiral, sir," the man saluted. "Sir, it appears we have a stowaway on board."

Stowaway? How could that happen? They were so careful when loading their guests and all their luggage.

Admiral Esrith set his drink down, stood and walked toward him. "How do you know this, Ensign?"

"Sir, he was found on a routine patrol, hidden in one of the wedge ships."

"Where is he now, Ensign?"

"He's locked in the brig, sir."

"Very good, Ensign. Tell Captain Melbus I will be there shortly."

"Yes, Admiral." He saluted, then left.

Admiral Esrith returned to his drink. "To unencumbered," he said and finished off his drink.

"Sir, it's possible he may be an Earthen who stowed away," Keely said. She finished her drink.

"Yes, that's very possible, unless it's another alien race."

"Another alien race, sir?" Keely asked.

"Yes. You don't think the greys are the only aliens interested in your planet, do you?"

"After what happened recently on Earth with the 'Black Government' being exposed, I can believe anything."

The admiral glanced at Gadara and Eno. "You two stay here." Then he glanced at Tremol and Keely. "You two, come with me." He headed out the door.

Keely tried to keep up with the admiral's long strides. Tremol had no problem. She knew he was 6'2", but Esrith seemed taller. Her shorter frame had to compensate by trotting behind them.

When they arrived on the brig, there stood an Air Force officer, behind bars. He was about the same height as Esrith, maybe a little taller, with brown hair and eyes. Not as good looking as her Tremol, but not bad to look at.

"How did you get on board this ship?" the admiral demanded.

"The same as everyone else," he replied.

"Who are you and who do you work for?" she asked.

"I'm Torin Conolly, Astronaut of the U.S. Space Force."

"The President just started the Space Force, how can you be an Astronaut of the U.S. Space Force?" she demanded.

"The Space Force has been around since before you were born," Conolly said. "The President just made it official by going public with it."

That was odd. Her father had mentioned the same thing about the Space Force, but she thought it was just a conspiracy. She pulled up the Comm-Pad and scrolled down the list of Americans who boarded the ship with her and Tremol. "I don't see your name on this list," she said.

"Yes, and I don't remember seeing you board our transporter before we took off." Tremol crossed his arms, waiting for an answer.

"I was one of the first who boarded your ship. I gave you the name Smith."

"Smith?" Tremol asked. He glanced over Keely's shoulder.

She looked up at him. "Yes, we do have a Smith on the list."

"Why did you give us a fake name? Or is Conolly your real name?" Tremol asked.

"My name is Torin Conolly. Smith couldn't make it and there was no time to change anything, so I took his place. No sense in wasting a trip to space, right?"

"What were you doing down on the flight deck?" Tremol said. His hands on his hips.

"I wanted to see how the ship felt with me in the cockpit."

Tremol glanced at Keely. "Cockpit?"

"You call it the Nav-U-Comm." She glanced at Conolly. "You had no business down there. We are all guests on this ship and we are responsible for all of you."

"Who sent you?" Tremol demanded.

"I get my orders from the NSA."

"We have someone here from the NSA," she said. "I'll check with him."

"The Joint Chiefs of Staff are here to purchase some of the ships the Vaedrans have. I'm here to learn to fly those ships so I can train other astronauts to fly them." Conolly said.

The admiral gestured for all of them to leave. The three of them stepped out into the hallway.

"Do you believe him?" the admiral asked.

"I don't know. I feel something is off." She craned her neck to look up at him. "We should have been informed," she said.

"I agree." Tremol said.

"Let's go back to the lounge. I'll share an idea I have with you. Afterward, you two question your other guests to see if anyone knows Conolly, then fill me in on the results."

The admiral led them back to the lounge. Once inside, the five of them gathered at a booth. "Bring us all a round of Detonators," he said to the barkeep.

Esrith glanced around the table at each person, then stopped his gaze at her.

"I did speak to your President with both Councilors Thebes and Contor present. He was concerned that this 'shadow government' that was exposed during the abduction of our landing party, would try to get a hold of our technology, without sharing it with the rest of the government or the world."

"Did he mention Mr. Conolly?" she asked.

"No, he did not." Esrith said.

"I say, toss him out into space," Gadara responded.

All heads turned toward her.

"That's a little harsh, even for you, Captain Gadara," Admiral Esrith said.

"He's a stowaway."

"He should be locked up," Eno said.

"He was actually on our list," Keely said. "We just didn't remember him."

"I have a better idea," the admiral said.

Everyone turned toward the admiral. "Captain Gadara will train him to fly our cruisers, while pumping him for information and keeping an eye on him."

"Sir?" Captain Gadara's mouth hung open. "He will be exposed to all the technical and sensitive information concerning our ships. Won't that be dangerous?"

"I think so too, sir." Eno said. "We can't trust him. He's already been in a sensitive area of the ship."

The barkeep returned with the drinks. "I suggest you take a drink, Gadara." the admiral said. After he reached for a drink, everyone followed suit.

"I know you were about to finish up your last class, so you can move into Special Missions, Captain, the admiral began.

"Special Missions, sir?" Tremol sat forward.

"Yes. I know you both wanted the same position, Tremol, but the President just created a new position for you and Keely. This will be an important mission for future trips with delegates from both systems. Right now, they are from your government, Keely, but the President said he will share this with other nations, so there will be interested people for years to come."

Tremol glanced at her and she smiled. A tinge of excitement ran through her.

"In the meantime, Eno will befriend this Conolly to get into his head and find out what he is really doing here, while Gadara trains him. Both of you will keep an eye on him and report to me."

Gadara got the barkeep's attention. "Another Detonator."

"I'll have another one, too," Eno said.

"Anyone else?" The barkeep asked. The admiral, Tremol and she raised their glasses. "Yes!" they said in unison.

After finishing her third drink, she realized she was on the verge of tipsy and motioned to Tremol it was time to leave. The two of them headed out into the hall. She leaned against the wall to steady herself. "Wow, those drinks were potent. I'm going to need help getting back to the room."

Tremol laughed and offered her his arm for support. "I guess your shortness has something to do with how you handle the drinks."

"Aren't you feeling a little bit tipsy?"

"No, but a fourth drink would move me in that direction."

They walked toward the people mover. "I can't believe Conolly was able to sneak around the flight deck without being seen." She glanced up at him and felt dizzy.

"Yes, that was pretty presumptuous of him. However, he was caught, which means the Concordance staff is always on alert and monitoring this ship." Tremol said.

"Exactly!" She pushed the button on the panel to call for the people mover. "First we'll speak to Mr. Porter," she said, suddenly feeling very relaxed as they stepped into the people mover.

"Is he the NSA person?" Tremol asked.

"Yes." She nodded and felt dizzy from the movement. "Then we'll speak to the Joint Sheefs of Thaff." Did she just slur her words? The effects of the three drinks hit her hard.

Tremol pushed a button on the people mover. When the door hissed open, he led her to their room.

"I thought we were going to see Mr. Porter?" she asked, once they were inside the room.

"Change of plans." He lifted her chin and gave her a passionate kiss. She wrapped her arms around him and pulled him toward the bed.

"I like this idea better," she said.

"The Earth pilots were quick to learn the Nav-U-Comm, but without our ships to practice on, they may forget everything they learned." Eno said.

"Did they do moon landings?" Gadara asked.

"No, but a couple of them talked about it. They use rockets to get there and it takes them a long time to build one and have it ready. Their space station sounds small and cramped, unlike our stations."

"It sounds as if we have more to offer them, than they can offer us." Gadara said.

"That's what I think as well."

Gadara took the last sip of her third Detonator. "I think I'll call it a night. I've got reports to do on my pilot trainees."

"That sounds like fun."

Gadara stood up. "*This* has been fun." She glanced at Eno. "And it looks like you're getting a new quarters mate."

Eno's smile faded immediately.

Gadara headed toward the brig to meet the Earthen who would change her training plans. No one had ever gotten through the flight course in less than five weeks. She worked it out to six weeks to give them extra flight time. But since they were space bound, there would be no landings until they got to Vestra Major. She would have to adjust everything to fit within six days. She would not compromise her standards. This man better be worth her valuable time.

"Captain Gadara!" The guard saluted when she approached the brig.

"Where is the stowaway?" she demanded.

The guard led her to the cell, where a strangely dressed man sat on a bunk in the small space. He stood immediately when he spotted her. He slowly looked her up and down, so she returned the gaze. He was pleasant to look upon, but looks like his were deceiving.

"What is your name?" she demanded.

"Conolly. Torin Conolly."

She gave him her 'don't mess with me' stare. "What is your purpose here?"

"I'm here to learn how to fly your ships so I can train others back home."

"Where is home?"

"Earth."

She leaned closer to the bars. "Where were you when Lieutenant Eno trained your pilots?"

"I was not aware anyone trained our pilots."

"Don't you work for the Earthen military?"

"I'm an astronaut with the U.S. Space Force."

"Why do you want to learn to fly our ships?"

"I told you, to teach others how to fly these ships."

"That's not why. That's what. Tell me why or you can sit there until we return to Earth."

"All right!" He looked down then back into her eyes. His demeanor changed somewhat. "I get a promotion if I do this."

"What kind of promotion?"

"Moon Base Commander," he mumbled.

She glared at him. This reasoning did not make sense. He would be promoted to a high-ranking position and all he had to do was learn to fly their ships? What kind of leader was he? What kind of training did he already have to be a Commander?

"What is your rank?"

"I'm an Astronaut, I told you."

"What is an astronaut?"

"A pilot, of sorts. I'm a damn good pilot and a test pilot, too."

"Have you led any missions?"

"No."

"Why do you want to be a Commander when you have no experience?"

"That's the deal I made when I left." He glanced down at his feet.

"They lied to you." She turned and walked away.

"Wait!" he called out.

She stopped in her tracks, waiting for his next words.

"I want to **become** a Moon Base Commander, but my promotion is for Lieutenant."

She turned and marched back to the cell. "I do not tolerate liars or laziness. If you want to fly our ships, you have six days to learn what I teach in six weeks. Are you in or out?"

"I'm in."

She turned to the guard. "Release him to me."

"Yes, Captain."

"Captain?" Conolly's eyes widened.

The guard unlocked the cage and Conolly stepped out, eyeing the insignia on her white flight suit.

"Thank you, Captain," Conolly said.

"Follow me." She led him to the people mover and headed to deck 6. She remained silent, while she thought of all the work she had to do tonight. It was already getting late, and the drinks were affecting her.

"How long have you been flying, Captain?" Conolly asked, breaking the long silence.

"Since I was a child." This man better be worth the effort or she would remain a Captain for a lot longer than she wanted.

When the people mover stopped, she exited onto deck 6 and headed to the room at the end of the hall.

She knocked on the door. Conolly stood beside her without speaking. The man had at least seven inches on her.

The door hissed open. Eno stood in the doorway.

"Hello Lieutenant Eno, this is Astronaut Torin Conolly of the U.S. Space Force. He will be your new quarters mate for the duration of our trip. Have him at our Sim room at 0900 hours." She saluted Eno, and Eno returned the salute. She turned and left the two men in the hall.

"Hello and welcome aboard," Eno reached his hand out to Conolly. "My name is Eno ni Esrith, but you can call me Eno."

Conolly shook his hand. "On Earth, the military goes by our last name, but you can call me Torin. Does everyone go by their first names here?"

"Yes." Eno stepped aside so he could enter.

He glanced around the small area. Against the far wall was a set of bunk beds with a type of cabinet at the end. Across from the bunks was a door to a small compartment. A desk squeezed into the corner between the bunks and the compartment, with a chair and a lamp of sorts on the desk top. "Nice quarters."

"Thanks. I tried to make it as homey as I could."

Eno pointed to the top bunk. "That one is yours. And you can use the last two drawers of the clothes cabinet."

"What is that?" He pointed to the other door in the room.

"That's our cleansing compartment. We're the only ones on this deck who have one. Everyone else has to use the community cleansing compartments." Eno opened the door so he could see the inside. It appeared to be a large port-a-toilet with a shower overhead.

"Nice. How did you manage to get one of those?"

"We had an odd number of men on this trip, and I'm the admiral's son."

"His son? That explains the resemblance."

"Yes, sometimes being his son has its perks and sometimes it's a burden."

"I get it." He glanced around the room once more.

"Did you bring any clothes with you?" Eno asked.

"No, actually. I came at the last minute."

"Well, Captain Gadara expects you at 0900 hours, so you'll need to either wear what you have on, or we'll have to borrow some clothes."

"I'll wear these again tomorrow and find something else when the class is over."

"You know what you're in for, don't you?"

"I'm a fast learner."

"For your sake, I hope so."

He thought about her name. Gadara. Unusual to say the least, but her looks were exceptional. That long dark-brown hair, pulled back in a braid, set off her exotic features. He bet she looked even more provocative with her hair down. Something about her made him want to learn more. Well, he would have exactly six days to do that.

❄   3   ❄

The next morning, Keely woke up next to Tremol, his bare arms wrapped around her naked body. She blinked a few times, trying to get the fog out of her head.

"Tremol?" She shook him.

"Hmmm?"

"I don't remember getting here last night."

"I know." He pulled her closer. "You were quite inebriated." He kissed her forehead.

"Did we speak to Mr. Porter?"

"No. I felt it would be better to speak to him when you are clear headed."

"Did I make of fool of myself?"

"No, but you are less inhibited with me after having three Detonators."

"Was that a good thing?"

"Oh yes. Yes it was." He kissed her deeply and she returned the passion.

〜

An hour later, the two of them headed to deck 5 where all the Earth Delegates were quartered.

Tremol knocked on Claud Porter's door.

"Yes?" Porter said, opening his door.

He was about mid-fifties, not quite six feet tall, with grayish-brown hair and brown eyes. He took off his glasses, wiped the lenses clean with a cloth he later pocketed, and returned them to his face.

"Mr. Porter, we are the liaisons for the Earthen Delegation," Keely began.

"Yes, I know who you two are." He stepped outside his door, pressing the hold open button. "What do you want?"

"We have some questions for you Mr. Porter." Tremol crossed his arms again.

"And what are those?"

"Did you come on board on behalf of the NSA?" she asked.

"Yes."

"Did you see anyone getting on board after we went inside the Nav-U-Comm?" Tremol asked.

"The what?"

"The cockpit," she said.

"No. Was I supposed to?"

"So, you came alone?" Tremol asked.

"Of course! Do you think I sneaked someone on board this ship?"

"Did you, Mr. Porter?" she asked.

Porter's brows furrowed as he glared at her.

"Do you know Torin Conolly, Mr. Porter?" Tremol asked.

"No, but I know about him, why?"

"He said he works for you, Mr. Porter." she said.

"Not me, personally. He worked for NSA, NASA, and the U.S. Space Force. Why do you want to know?"

"Let's say he was an uninvited guest." Tremol said.

Porter shrugged. "Maybe not."

"Why do you say that. What do you know?"

"It's a need to know basis."

"Don't you think we need to know this information, Mr. Porter? Especially since we are responsible for the lives of all the Delegates from Earth?" Tremol asked.

"Is he here now, Mr. Tremol?"

"It's Lieutenant Tremol. And yes, that's why we are here."

"Well, now he's your problem." Claud Porter turned to enter his room.

Before he could step inside, Keely twisted his arm behind his back and shoved him hard against the wall. She whispered harshly beside his ear, "Let me remind you, Mr. Porter, that I am with the Secret Service and I consider *you* my problem as well." She pulled him away from the wall and shoved him into his room.

Tremol hit the door panel, shutting the door, and placed an object on the outside. "Until we figure this out, Mr. Porter, you are confined to your room. Your meals will be brought to you."

"What is that?" she asked.

"It's an unlocking disruptor. He won't be able to open his door from the inside and no one can open it from the outside until I remove it."

Claud Porter banged on his door and yelled. "Is this the way you treat all your guests?"

"Yes, when we feel we've been lied to and they have questionable intentions," Tremol answered.

"Can anyone else remove it?" Keely asked as they walked away.

"No. It's got my code and no one else knows it but me."

"Cool. Now let's go talk to the Joint Chiefs of Staff."

He led Keely away and down the hall. She looked over the list of guests who made up the new Earth Delegation. "There's a representative from each of the major executive departments here," she said. "Plus, some people from government agencies. Twenty-three in all."

"When we get near the Vaedra system, I will contact the Council and set up meetings. They can ask all the questions they want."

"Do you have similar agencies or departments in your government?" She handed the Comm-Pad to Tremol.

He glanced over it. "No. We keep things simple. Each tribe, clan, or community has a representative. They meet on their respective planets twice an ano to discuss any concerns. If something comes up, they can call a special meeting, but that's up to each planet. Then, once an ano, two people from each planet are chosen from the representatives they have and they meet on Vestra Major. They bring up trade and any other significant concerns and discuss it there."

"Who pays for all of this?" Keely asked.

"No one gets paid. It's all voluntary. However, each tribe, clan, or community will collect kashis for their representative to travel to Vestra Major or to the capital of that planet."

"Wow. All of these people," she pointed to the list, "get paid to travel and work for these departments or agencies."

"Who pays for those people?" he asked.

"The taxpayers."

"What is that?"

"We, the people. I'll have to give you a history lesson on just the U.S.A. All the countries of our world, on Earth, have different governments, so it's different everywhere."

"It sounds complicated," he said.

"Oh, it is."

Tremol ushered her toward the mess deck for the morning meal. "We will check with the others after we eat."

"Good idea. The admiral needs to know we are dealing not only with a stowaway, but a guest with secrets."

The Concordance was larger than any battleship she had ever seen, even the newer ones. But it didn't look like a ship and it didn't look like any plane, either. It was more like a city with its shops and offices. There were the smaller space craft and their pilots and all the people responsible for the maintenance and upkeep, plus the people required to manage this big ship.

"How do your people pay for its military?" she asked.

"Through trade. Each community, clan, or tribe sells or trades goods or services to provide for their communities. A portion of that is used for the upkeep of the military."

"Oh, sort of like a tax."

Tremol glanced down at her. "Ah, maybe so. We'll have to discuss this more on a full stomach. I can't think clearly when my stomach makes these noises."

Tremol pushed the button on the mess hall door and it hissed open. "This is the eating hall," he said.

"Well, that makes sense." There were rows upon rows of tables with benches attached. It was set up cafeteria style, with a few people setting plates of food out at a long counter.

She slipped the straps of the Comm-Pad across her chest and over her shoulder so she could use both hands. Tremol escorted her to the line and they each grabbed a tray. There was a variety of food on plates, on display. She watched Tremol take something and she followed suit. After grabbing some liquid that looked like coffee, the two headed to some empty seats.

"What is this drink?" she asked.

"Capu. I think you call it coffee."

She took a sip. "Yes, and it needs some cream."

"I'll get it." Tremol was up and headed toward the line. He grabbed something out of a container and brought it back to the table.

"Thank you." She poured the liquid into her capu, then sipped. It was close enough. It didn't taste exactly like coffee with cream, but it would do. "I hope this has caffeine in it."

"Ah, the stuff that helps you wake up. Yes, indeed."

Keely glanced around and noticed everyone wore the same white outfits. "Are they all military people?"

"Yes. That's why we came in early. We'll go back and bring our guests here to eat in a few minutes. The military should all be finished by then."

"Is that why you wore your uniform?" she asked.

"We call it a unicrin. I had no other clothes with me on this trip. I'm what you call quasi-military, law enforcement."

"Oh?"

"I enforce the laws in space, between the planets, hence, I work for the Interplanetary Space Patrol. All the others are here to enforce peace among our planets and neighboring systems, so they would be military. When something happens that is bigger than our agency can handle, we call in the military."

"Do each of your planets have law enforcement on the planet itself?"

"Yes, of course. Depending on the planets, though, they each have their own names for their law enforcement agency. On Vestra Major, we call them Law Patrol. They patrol the streets and roadways of the cities and countryside, making people feel safe in their neighborhoods."

"And how do you pay for these people?" She asked.

"Each person who works for a wage must give a portion to the city for expenses like that."

"So, you do have taxes."

"We call it apportionment."

"Same thing, different name." She glanced at her watch. "Should we get our guests?"

"Yes. The eating hall is clearing out. Let me see that list."

Keely took the Comm-Pad off her shoulder and handed it to Tremol.

Tremol powered it on and looked over the list.

"Looks like all twenty-three were assigned to the same deck with some of them doubling up. This should be easy."

The two of them headed to deck 5, where they knocked on each door.

"Meet us in the eating hall, deck 2, in thirty minutes."

❄   4   ❄

Eno's alarm went off early.

"Arise and seize the day!" Eno said to his new quarters mate.

Conolly opened one eye and saw Eno smiling at him. He blinked awake. "Are you always this happy in the morning?"

"I try. Every day is an adventure, don't you think?"

He sat up and rubbed his head. "Yes, actually I do."

"First up, first in," Eno said.

"What does that mean?"

"First in the cleansing compartment." Eno hung up a flight suit outside the compartment door on one side, and a towel on the other, then stepped his bare ass into the cleansing room.

Hmmm. Eno either slept in the nude, or removed his skivvies before he went in. Conolly glanced over the edge of the bed. No skivvies on the floor. He'd have to ask where to put his dirty laundry once he got something clean to wear.

He slowly crawled out of the bunk, remembering not to lift his head. He'd hit his head several times the night before, trying to get into the bed. There wasn't much head space on the top bunk for someone his size, but there was plenty on the bottom. Come to think of it, even Gadara was over six foot tall. He wondered if all the Vaedran people were over six foot.

He opened the cabinet where he would put his clothes, if he had any, and saw a bag hanging from a small hook on one side. Eno's three flight suits were folded neatly in one drawer. No socks or skivvies. He closed the compartment and stretched.

Eno reached out from the cleansing compartment and grabbed his towel. Shortly after, he stepped out, naked, and put on his navy-blue flight suit.

"It's too wet to change in there," Eno said.

"I bet. You should see our bathrooms on Earth." He grabbed his shirt and pants.

"What's a bath room?"

"Well, a little more sophisticated than a cleansing compartment, but in space, this is better than what we had on our space station and rockets."

"I'd like to see that one day," Eno said.

He hung up his clothes. "Trust me, this is much better." He turned around, looking for a towel.

"Here you go," Eno said. He opened a drawer in the cleansing compartment, where there were several large bath towels.

"What do you use for soap or shampoo?" Conolly asked.

Eno pointed to the nozzle over the toilet and then to the buttons on the wall behind it. "The water temperature is pre-set, but that button is for water only, the other is for cleanser. The cleanser is used for both hair and body."

"Got it. Thanks." He removed his skivvies and stepped inside. Once he relieved himself, he turned on the water. The spray was just the way he liked it. Once he was wet, he tried the soap button. He got enough all over and washed his hair. Then he used the water button again to rinse off.

This was nice. NASA needed this setup. It was simple and easy to use. Once he dried off, he pulled his skivvies off the hook and put them on again, then stepped out to dress.

Eno combed his hair while he dressed.

"What about a toothbrush and toothpaste? Do you think we can find an extra? I don't think I can go another day without brushing my teeth," he said.

"Sure, I'll see if I can round one up for you. But first, I'm starving."

He pulled a comb out of his back pocket and ran it through his hair, then slipped his socks and shoes back on.

"Okay. Ready."

They stepped out into the hall, heading for the elevator.

"Do all pilots wear the navy-blue uniform?" he asked.

"These are called unicrins and yes, pilots wear navy-blue. Officers wear white. I have a white unicrin but it's dirty. That's only for official ceremonies, though. The guards wear a medium gray, the techs wear a light gray, all other personnel wear black unicrins."

"And do all these unicrins look like flight suits? Like yours?"

"Yes. And what kind of unicrin are you wearing?"

"This is an Air Force uniform. I'll be changing to the Space Force uniform when I get back. They're in the process of designing them now."

"Space Force? Is that like our Star Force?"

"Is that what you call your military branch?" he asked.

"We have Star Force, Land Force, and Sea Force branches. The Land and Sea forces cover everything on the planet, with each planet having their own. The Star Force is shared by all the planets. We also have an Interplanetary

Space Patrol that patrols between the planets, keeping the peace and law. They are a quasi-military group and their unicrins are white, but they have different insignias on their left chest."

"So what colors do the Land Force and Sea Force wear?"

"The Land Force wears green and the Sea Force wears a bluish-green."

When they arrived at the elevator, Eno pushed the button. "We call these people movers."

"Makes sense. Much faster than what we have on Earth, too."

"I'll give you a quick tour on our way to the eating hall."

"Sounds good to me."

The door to the people mover opened and they stepped inside.

"We were just on deck 6 where most of the pilots stay. Below that is where the cruisers are parked and where you were found, along with the Space techs, engines, and the brig, otherwise known as deck 7. Above us, on deck 5, is where all the delegates are staying. You would be there, but the quarters were full."

"Last minute plans, you know." He shrugged. All he remembered was he needed to be on that transporter before they took off, not five minutes before he saw the thing.

"Well, on deck 4, we have the Med Bay, Fitness, Laundry, and Ancillary. After we eat, we'll go to Ancillary and see if we can find you a toothbrush."

"Great!"

"On deck 3, we have crew members only, but on deck 2, we have some crew and the eating hall." The people mover stopped and they got out.

"Perfect timing," he said.

As the two of them walked toward the eating hall, he thought he got a glimpse of Gadara.

"Deck 1 is reserved for officers and some guests, but in the center of that is the Bridge, which is slightly raised."

"Sounds interesting."

The two of them got in line to grab something to eat. He glanced around and noticed a lot of people dressed in black unicrins with some in the pilot garb. There were a few guards sprinkled around the room but they weren't eating.

"Where do the officers eat?" He asked.

"We eat over there." Eno gestured to a far wall with a large glass window. Inside, he could see Gadara, sitting by herself and eating.

"Does she always eat alone?" he asked.

"Who?"

"Gadara."

"Don't let her hear you call her that. Make sure you say Captain Gadara. She earned that rank and she will let you know that."

"Does she?"

"Sometimes I'll sit with her, unless some of the pilots catch up to me. I like to eat early."

He thought it was sad that such a beautiful woman had to eat alone. "What kind of captain is she?"

"She's tough. She's got high standards and you'll have to meet them or she won't pass you."

They both grabbed a tray and started loading up food. He followed Eno to a table and they sat across from each other. He managed to sit where he could see Gadara.

"Is Captain Gadara the only flight instructor on this ship?"

"Yes. And she's trained all of us but Captain Melbus, the

Ensign, and my father, of course. They transferred from another ship."

"Mmmm. This is good," he said. Neither of them spoke again until they finished eating.

"Come on, I'll show you what to do with your tray." Eno stood and led the way to the entrance. He pointed to a stack of trays and a trash can of sorts. He followed suit and left the eating hall with Eno.

Eno motioned to the community cleansing compartments across from the eating hall. One had a figure of a woman and the other, a man. So much like Earth.

Eno glanced at his watch. "We have time to go to Ancillary, if you want?"

"Sure."

Once they got there, he was able to look around. "How much do they charge for a toothbrush and toothpaste?"

"A credit, I think."

He reached into his pockets and pulled out a couple dollars and some change.

"Uh, that's not going to work." Eno took the toothbrush and the container of paste from him and went to the cashier. "Here, put this on my tab," Eno said to her.

"Thanks! I owe you."

"Think nothing of it. But as far as a unicrin of some sort, that's different. We have a meeting later this morning. I'll check on it."

"You've been really helpful. Thanks!"

They headed back to the room so he could brush his teeth.

"I forgot to tell you, we have a curfew at 0000 hours.

"A curfew? Why?"

"It's ship-wide. The admiral believes everyone should get plenty of sleep so they are ready to go at a moment's notice."

"What if you get caught?"

"Well, you get written up and then locked up for twenty-four hours."

"That's harsh."

"Admiral's orders and they apply to me, too."

Eno glanced at his watch again. "We just have enough time to get you to the Sim Room. Let's go."

They headed out the door. Eno jogged, so he joined him.

"Are we late?"

"We'll take the stairs. They are much faster."

He followed Eno up the circular stairwell to deck 4. Just around the corner from the Ancillary was the Sim Room.

"Here you go, with a couple minutes to spare. Good luck."

Eno gave a salute and he returned it.

As he pressed the door button, thinking he was early, there was Captain Gadara at the front of the room, leaning against a wall, glancing at her watch.

5

"Punctual. That's one point in your favor. Sit here." She pointed to a console at the front.

The door hissed closed and while Conolly moved to sit at the console, she handed him a Comm-Pad. "I hope you're a fast reader. When you finish this manual, we'll go over the simulators."

"Yes, ma'am," he said.

"It's Captain Gadara to you," she admonished him.

"Yes, Captain Gadara." He looked up at her and she held his gaze, with her 'I mean business' stare. But for a brief second, something passed between them. She looked away and headed for her desk in the back of the class. She couldn't put her finger on it, but she felt something. Was it a challenge?

She glanced over the work she still had to do to finish preparing for a short, fast version of this class, when she thought she heard the touch of his finger against the Comm-Pad screen. She glanced up and noticed he was bent over the device, but she could hear him tapping the screen every few seconds. Maybe he *was* a fast learner.

She glanced at her chrono. It took most students a week to finish the lessons. Then she tested them before she let them practice on the simulators. Once they passed all those tests, then she let them fly, with two weeks total for each ship. Their flight time depended on how fast they finished the lessons and sim work.

At the rate he's going, they just might start the simulator tomorrow. But this is the rate they would have to move to complete all this work in six days. Her promotion depended on him.

She glanced at her chrono again. Time to head to the morning briefing at 0930. The officers met in the Map Room which was the largest room besides the eating hall. She was anxious to compare notes with Eno to see what he found out.

Admiral Esrith addressed the group. "Some of you are already aware of our stowaway problem. He claims he's an astronaut in the U.S. Space Force from Earth. He says his reason for being here is to learn how to fly our ships so he can teach others back on Earth."

Captain Melbus interrupted. "Do you think he has other intentions, sir?"

"Yes I do. His president, a leader from the U.S. Government, warned me of a shadow government that may try to steal our technologies or military secrets and not share them with the U.S. Government," the admiral said.

"What are we going to do with him, sir?" Another officer asked.

"That's a good question. Captain Gadara is teaching him how to fly our ships while trying to learn his real purpose here. She and Lieutenant Eno are also monitoring his activities, and together, they will report to me on his actions." He glanced at her. "Captain Gadara, do you have anything to report this morning?"

"Yes, Admiral. I've enlisted the help of Lieutenant Eno as his quarters mate and mentor, to find out anything I may not be able to learn. A few minutes ago, I set him up with a Comm-Pad to read the manuals." She caught Eno's attention. "Lieutenant? Do you have anything to report?"

"Yes Captain Gadara. He mentioned that he came on board at the last minute, so he has no change of clothes or necessities to get him through the next few days in space."

"Take care of that, Lieutenant Eno, and thank you."

"Yes, Admiral." Eno sat down, so she did too.

"I want the rest of you to report anything unusual about him or his actions to Captain Gadara," the admiral said.

Since nothing else was reported, the admiral sent us on our way. Gadara hurried to the Sim Room and found Conolly still reading.

She worked on her program for a while until she finally realized she was hungry. She glanced at her chrono. 1100 hours. She stood and stretched. "You can take a thirty-minute meal break, Astronaut Torin Conolly."

Conolly stood and powered down the Comm-Pad. He stretched as well and walked toward her. "Thank you, Captain Gadara. On Earth, the military uses our last names when addressing us. You can call me Conolly, since I'm not an officer yet. But if you want to get personal, you can call me Torin." He flashed her a smile that took her off guard.

She blinked momentarily, then grabbed his arm, turning him to face her. "In the Vaedran Military, unless you are an officer, you don't get personal with anyone. Understand, Conolly?"

"Yes, Captain Gadara. I was just making a joke."

She released her grasp. "You may go."

He looked right at her. "Yes, Captain Gadara."

There it was again. He challenged her with his eyes. He finally looked away and headed to the door.

Conolly managed to find the mess hall. What did Eno call it? Oh, yeah, the eating hall. That made sense. He had to eat and get back before 11:30.

After pissing off the captain, he wanted to stay on her good side. At least she liked punctuality. He wondered what else she liked.

The line moved quickly and he managed to find a seat at the end of a long table. When he sat down, the rest of the people around him stared. All of them wore flight suits. Some were navy blue, while others were light gray and some were black.

Across the hall, he saw Captain Gadara go into the Officer's eating hall. He ate quickly, then returned his tray to the stack beside the door. He went in search of a toilet. Eno had called it a cleansing compartment. And there it was, right in front of him.

This was the community cleansing compartment where there were several stalls. Very private and functional as each one was like the one in their room with the exception of a cabinet to hold clothing, to keep it dry while they showered. There were five compartments to a side.

Too bad NASA didn't have anything like this. Then again, NASA would want a ship like this instead of their rockets. This was superior and more efficient than anything NASA had.

He headed back to the Sim Room. If he kept up this pace,

he would finish the lesson by this afternoon. So far, the Vaedran manual had similarities to the greys' ships he'd flown.

When he entered the room, Gadara was not there. He glanced at his watch. He had five minutes on her. He sat down, powered up the device, and picked up reading where he'd left off. His head started pounding, so he pinched the skin above his brows. He didn't remember having headaches in his early years, but lately, they had become more frequent. A minute later, the door hissed open. He glanced over his shoulder to catch her trying to hide a smile. Now, he knew what he wanted to do. He turned back and continued reading.

Gadara sat at her desk in the back of the room. Conolly had impressed her twice with his punctuality. He almost caught her in a smile, something she tried hard not to show to any student. But since he had gotten through half the manual in the first half of class, she wondered if she should expect more from the rest of her class. Or maybe he was just exceptional. His smile certainly was, or she wouldn't have been caught off guard.

She finished her reports from the last flight test of the other student pilots. She had one more day before they returned to class. They had to do sim work on landing at a space station. Conolly might benefit from that, even though he couldn't do any landings until they reached Timucan. Then, they could fly down to Vestra Major and practice land-ings there.

She looked up from her paperwork to see Conolly standing in front of her.

"Excuse me, Captain Gadara, but I've finished reading

the manual."

Surprised and impressed, she checked her chrono to recompose herself. It was 0520. She stood. "You can have a thirty-minute break, then report back here for some sim training."

"Yes, Captain Gadara." He saluted and kept her gaze until she returned the salute. Then he left.

She sat down in shock. This was so unusual, yet this is exactly the pace she needed to get her promotion. She opened her cabinet and pulled out a Comm-Pad and set up the test for the wedge ships she would administer when he returned. This would tell her what he remembered and whether or not she would allow him to practice on the simulators. Then she went to the front of the room and programmed the simulator for the wedge ships as well. If he passed this test and finished the simulator work tonight, she would take him out in the ship tomorrow.

She glanced at her chrono. She didn't have time to eat, unless she grabbed something and brought it back to the room. She dashed out the door. Partway down the hall, she saw Conolly returning with a food container in one hand and a drink container in the other. Oh, no. The eating hall must be full.

"I didn't see you in the eating hall, Captain Gadara, so I brought you something back." He handed her the food container and drink.

"Oh, I…thank you." She was never at a loss for words, but no one had ever gone out of their way to do something like this for her before.

"I'm anxious to get through these lessons, aren't you?" He looked hopeful and excited.

"Why, yes."

He walked ahead and opened the door for her. She was

thrown off guard again. Why did he keep doing that?

She walked into the room and set the food down on her desk. "Here." She handed him the Comm-Pad. "Take this to your desk and complete the test. Afterward, you will do the simulator work."

"Yes Captain Gadara." He took the Comm-Pad back to his desk and started the test.

She ate her meal, wondering if all Earthen men acted like him. His behavior felt odd. By the time she finished her meal, he returned to her desk with the Comm-Pad.

"Did you have a question, Conolly?"

"Yes, Captain Gadara. What do I do when I'm finished?"

"What? Certainly you aren't finished yet?"

He handed her the Comm-Pad.

She scrolled through it, checking his answers to the one hundred questions. All of them were correct.

"I don't understand," she said, amazed at his skill.

"I'm a fast learner. I have a photographic memory."

"What does that mean?"

"It means I can remember in great detail things I've read or photographs I've looked at just once."

"Everything?"

"Pretty much."

"How long have you had this skill?"

"Since I was a child."

She stood and walked over to the simulator. He followed her. "Sit here and do this sim work. There are at least five scenarios in here that I want you to master. You can re-start them here, if you make a mistake." She pointed to a panel. "It will record your responses so I can see them. When you finish, let me know."

"Yes Captain Gadara."

Each scenario would take twenty to thirty minutes,

depending on how many re-starts he had. After that, she'd call it a night. She was excited and amazed at the same time, but she needed to clear something up with the admiral.

While Conolly worked on the simulator, she slipped out of the room.

~

She found the admiral in the Officers Lounge. The room was crowded tonight. She made her way to his table, which included Lieutenant Tremol and Keely.

"Tell me what you know about photographic memory," she asked the admiral.

"I've never heard of that," he answered.

Keely leaned forward. "I know something about that," she said.

Everyone turned toward Keely. "Go on," the admiral said.

"It's when a person can recall images or pages of texts after reading them."

"You have people on Earth who have that skill?"

"They say it's a myth, but I've seen agents in the Secret Service who can remember a great deal of information after viewing it once. And I've heard of those working in Intelligence who have an ability to recall a lot of information."

"Why do you ask?" Tremol glanced at Gadara.

"This Conolly read the manual in less than eight hours, then finished the test in thirty minutes. Now he's working on the simulator."

The barkeep brought a tray of drinks for the three of them.

"Have a drink with us, Captain," the admiral said.

"I would love to but I'm in teaching mode." She stood and left them to their amusements.

She slipped back into the Sim Room and sat in the back. She monitored Conolly's progress on her desktop. So far, he'd completed two of the five missions without errors. She checked for re-starts, but he had none. Conolly was turning out to be one of her best students.

By the time he finished all five simulations, she had yawned at least ten times. Her late-night drinking the day before had caught up with her.

She stood and stretched. "Great job for your first day," she said, walking toward him. "I've arranged for flight time tomorrow. Meet me here at 0900 hours."

"Yes Captain Gadara." He saluted and then left.

She was exhausted. She turned off the simulator and put up the Comm-Pad, then remembered her 0930 briefing in the morning. There was no point in meeting earlier.

She had to catch him. She raced down the hall, but he was gone. She was too tired to run the stairs, so she took a people mover. Once on his floor, she raced down the hall to his room and pressed the buzzer.

The door hissed open and Conolly stood in the doorway, without a shirt on. He was well built, but had hair on his chest, unlike Vaedran men. She tried not to stare, but it was hard.

"Hi Captain! Did you miss me already?"

Confused, she backed up. "No... I remembered I have a briefing at 0930. Let's meet in the Sim Room at 1030 tomorrow."

"Why yes, Captain Gadara, I'd love to."

She let her gaze fall from his eyes to his chest and abdomen and back up again. *Very nice.*

"Would you like to come in, Captain?"

"Uh, no. I'll see you in the morning."

"Good night, Captain Gadara." Then he winked.

❄ *6* ❄

no sat up in his bunk. "What was that about?"

"We're going to fly tomorrow." Conolly stuffed his shirt into the laundry bag Eno had given him.

"Yes, you told me that. But why did she show up here?"

"She changed our meeting time. Something about a briefing tomorrow morning."

"Hmm. She sounded a little confused to me," Eno said.

"Is she married?" he asked.

"Married? What is that?"

"You don't have marriage here?"

"I don't know what that is."

"You know, when a couple gets married and starts a family?"

"Oh, you mean does she have a mate?"

"A mate?"

"Yes, we call it taking a mate, and in the Vaedra system, we are mated for life."

"So, does she have a mate?"

"Captain Gadara does not have a mate. She's too busy teaching pilots to fly. She works all the time."

"That's a shame. She's beautiful."

"Don't let her hear you say that."

"Why?"

"She'll chastise you for it. I know, I've tried."

He stuffed his pants into the laundry bag and crawled up onto his bunk, in his skivvies. "Hey, thanks for the flight suit. Do you have any skivvies to go with it?"

"What's skivvies?"

"Underwear."

"I don't understand. We wear nothing under the flight suits."

"Commando! All right." That meant Gadara went commando as well. He smiled to himself, then rubbed his forehead where the dullness of the headache was easing up. A nice thought to sleep on.

The admiral leaned forward at the table. "So, you mean no one knows who this Torin Conolly is?"

"That's right, sir. Except the Joint Chiefs of Staff. They were vague with their answers, and were surprised to hear he was on board, learning to fly the ships." Tremol said.

"And they didn't expect to bring home ships at this time, either." Keely said.

"They said they would be ordering several to be delivered to Earth at a later date. However, Mr. Porter seems to know something about him, but he won't talk." Tremol added.

"So, we're back where we started."

"Yes sir," she said. "I did want to report that the delegates who are working with your people on board this ship are really impressed with your hospitality."

"That's good news. Thank you. I'll relate it to my staff."

"Well, Admiral, I think we'll call it a night," Tremol said as he stood. He reached his hand out to Keely and she took it.

"Good night, Admiral," she said, standing.

Gadara crawled into her bunk. What was happening to her? She acted confused around Conolly more than once today. Tomorrow, she had to be on her game. She had to be alert since she was teaching him how to fly. There was no way she could be confused while showing him maneuvers in the wedge ship. She closed her eyes, but all she could see was his smile. The smile that started her confusion. No one smiled at her. Ever. Then he winked. What did he mean by that? Was that an insult on Earth? Did he mean her harm?

Claud Porter paced back and forth in his room. He was now their prisoner. Well, he had five days to figure out how to escape. He picked up the alien object that controlled Conolly. All he had to do was whisper a command, and Conolly would obey. The greys could do it telepathically. He had to use the device they made for humans to control other humans.

The greys may have their faults, but they had some cool technology. The president thought he exposed the Black Government, but it would be a long time before they exposed everything that had been hidden over the years.

The next morning, Torin Conolly was awake before the alarm and headed for the cleansing compartment. First up, first in, according to Eno.

He hurriedly showered and dressed in the navy-blue flight suit Eno found for him. He was anxious to learn to fly the three Vaedran ships. As the cleansing compartment door hissed open, he saw Eno sitting up in bed, rubbing his eyes.

"A little eager today?" Eno asked.

"You could say that. Hey, how about finishing that tour of the ship this morning?"

"After we eat, I'll be glad to. But I have that same briefing at 0930 hours."

"It won't take that long, will it?"

"No, but it depends on how long it takes in the eating hall."

"You're wasting time! Get moving!"

Eno laughed while getting into the cleansing compartment.

Conolly combed his hair and studied his new unicrin, while waiting for Eno to finish. Rubbing his chin, he realized he needed a shave. He'd have to ask Eno for a razor later. Come to think of it, he didn't see a razor in the cleansing compartment.

He was eager today, but flying was his element. He had put up with this manual and sim practice just to fly these ships.

Once Eno was dressed and ready to go, they headed to the eating hall. Since they were earlier today, they moved through the line and finished eating with plenty of time for a tour.

"We'll take the stairs to deck 7," Eno said.

"Sure. I need the exercise. I'm off my routine here."

"Same here. I usually wake a little earlier and go to the Fitness Center and work out before eating. Since we left Earth's atmosphere, I haven't been able to get back to my routine either."

"Let's do that tomorrow," he said.

"Definitely."

Once they arrived on deck 7, everything seemed familiar.

"We call this the flight deck," Eno said.

The two of them stood on a bridge of sorts, looking down over a large, open area through thick, clear glass. On either side, there were two rows of ships. The lower row held the wedge-shaped ships. The row above held the wing ships.

"Beneath us, we have the transporters. They are used for either cargo or people. We have two of each. You'll get to fly those as well."

"That's what we arrived here on?"

"Yes."

"Today, I get to fly the wedge ship."

"Yes. Those are my favorite because they fly smooth and are used for fighting. They hold up to four people and are armed."

"What about the wing ships?"

"Those can hold up to two pilots and are also called military escorts. They are also armed and are the fastest and can outmaneuver the other two types of ships."

"Do I get a choice of which one I want to fly?"

"No. Captain Gadara will teach you on all three, provided you pass each of the manuals tests and sim work."

"You mean there's a manual for each one?"

"Yes and they get progressively harder. She won't pass you unless you can fly all three."

"I was supposed to fly back with one."

"The only ship that can make the trip from Vaedra to Earth is the transporter."

"That could be a problem."

"Why is that?"

"I was told I would be training others on one of those two ships." He pointed to the wedge and wing ships."

"So, are you here on behalf of your president?" Eno asked.

"I'm here on behalf of a higher authority."

Eno glanced at him but said nothing. How was he going to make the trip back to Earth in a ship that couldn't make the trip? Why couldn't the smaller ships make the trip? That's something that maybe Captain Gadara would tell him.

"This whole area is used for takeoffs and landings." Eno pointed to the space between all the rows of ships. "But behind us is where all the monitoring goes on." Eno turned around.

There were stations set up in a U shape behind them. Several people, dressed in light gray unicrins, worked the controls.

"They monitor everything operating on or around the ship including the smaller ships. We call them systems techs. They keep the ship operating smoothly, and when something goes wrong or breaks, they fix it."

"So how many people does it take to operate a ship this size?"

"Including the pilots, about 120. Right now, we have more than that on board with all the dignitaries and guests."

"What if you were in a war situation?"

"We've been able to stay out of war for decades, but in that case, we would have about four more escort ships and their crews, along with the fleet and their escort ships."

"How many ships in your fleet?"

"There are two star destroyers per planet, so about fourteen plus four extra escort ships each. Plus what we have on board this ship times fourteen."

"That sounds like a lot of fire power."

"This one ship can destroy a planet, so I think we've got plenty of fire power right here."

"Can we see the engines?"

"Since you're a visitor on this ship, they're off limits to you. Only certain Concordance personnel with security clearance can access the engines."

Conolly didn't know why he had asked those questions. Normally, he cared less about the engines or the details of a fleet. However, he felt *compelled* to ask them.

"Thanks for the tour." He patted Eno on the back.

"We'll take the people mover back." Eno glanced at his watch. "You've got a little time before meeting Captain Gadara. What will you do with yourself?"

"I don't know. Maybe check out the Ancillary again to kill time." *And look for a razor.*

＊   8   ＊

The admiral went around the table, asking everyone for their reports. Gadara didn't have much to add except the obvious, that Torin Conolly was ready to fly today.

"I have something to report," Lieutenant Eno said.

She sat up in her seat.

"I gave Conolly a tour of the flight deck this morning." He glanced at her and then the admiral. "He asked me a lot of questions about our ship, how many people were operating it, questions about war and preparation for war. But when we talked about the ships he will be flying, he was disappointed to learn that only the transporters could make the trip to Earth. He seems to think he will be flying one of the smaller ships back to Earth to train people. But when I asked him if his president sent him, he said he was here on a higher authority."

The admiral sat forward. "A higher authority?"

"Yes sir, that's what he said."

"I was told the president was the highest authority in his country," the admiral said.

"I was under the same impression," Eno said.

"Captain, a word with you after the meeting," the admiral said, glancing at her.

Great.

"The meeting is dismissed." The admiral stood.

She stood and walked toward him.

"Yes, sir?"

"Tremol and Keely reported to me last night that no one from the Earthen delegation knows Torin Conolly."

"I'm supposed to teach him how to fly the wedge ship today." She glanced at her chrono. She had fifteen minutes.

"Go ahead, but be on your guard. Let me know what you learn from him today."

"Yes, sir." She left and headed to the Sim Room.

"I think we need to speak to Mr. Porter once more," Keely said. She stepped outside their quarters with Tremol behind her.

"I think you're right. Maybe we can search his room."

"Why do you think that?" She glanced up at him.

"I don't trust him. I think he's hiding something, especially when no one knows him or Conolly."

"Well, the U.S. government is big. There are so many agencies in our government, it's possible they don't know each other."

"But shouldn't they at least know the name of the person?"

"I see your point." They stopped at the elevator the Vaedrans called a people mover. It worked more like the tubes used at the banks' drive-up windows and much faster.

"We'll ask him nicely and if he disagrees, he can stay in the brig while we search his room," Tremol said.

"He's a guest on this ship."

"But was he invited?"

"Well, his name was on the list with NSA beside it, so someone put him on the list." Keely picked up the Comm-Pad she wore across her chest. She pulled up the information.

"I have alerted security about searching his room. We need to get him out of it."

Keely glanced at her watch. "Well, it is time to eat. Maybe he will go with us willingly for that and we can give him a tour of the ship afterward."

"Great idea!" Tremol tapped his communicator on his shoulder. "Lieutenant Tremol to Lieutenant Gilbert."

"Go ahead."

"When you see me enter the eating hall with Porter, go ahead with the search."

"Yes, sir." Gilbert responded.

She pushed the button, calling for the people mover to go one deck down to Claud Porter's room.

When they arrived at his door, Tremol removed the 'unlocking disruptor' and knocked on it. He handed her the mechanism.

"Mr. Porter, we're here to give you a tour of our ship," he said.

"A tour? After being held a prisoner? Why would you do that?"

"Well, if you don't want the tour, we can leave you confined to your quarters as before, Mr. Porter," she said.

"Do you take me for a fool?" Porter asked.

"You can start by telling us the truth," Tremol said.

"The truth? The truth about what?"

"Why are you here, Mr. Porter?" she asked.

"I'm here just like the others, to meet my counterpart in the Vaedran government and share ideas and technology."

"Well, then, if you want to eat, come with us." Tremol motioned for Porter to join them. Porter glanced at both of them before reluctantly leaving with them.

Gadara opened the door to the Sim Room and there was Conolly. Early. Damn. She liked to be in the room before the students arrived. She motioned for him to come and he practically ran toward her. She didn't know whether to be amused or frightened at his eagerness.

She led him to the flight deck. "Do you remember the first thing you are to do once you board the ship?"

"Put on my harness, then familiarize myself with the Nav-U-Comm, before doing pre-flight."

"Very good." She led him down the steps to the ships. "We'll take my ship." She led him to the wedge ship.

"You have your own ship?"

"You would, too, if you were Vaedran Military."

"Yeah, that's not going to happen."

She gave him a side glance. Was that disappointment in his voice, or sarcasm? She pointed to the right side of the ship. "Get in over there."

He followed her orders.

Once inside, she put on her safety harness and glanced over at Conolly. He was already doing pre-flight. She smacked his hand. "Stop that."

He leaned a little close to her. "Are you getting personal with me, Captain Gadara?"

"What?" His comment threw her off.

"I'm not an officer, yet, but that felt a little personal to me." He winked at her.

Her heart skipped a beat. "Stop that!"

"Stop what? Pre-flight? I've already finished it. Let's see what this baby can do." He punched the Comm-link. "Permission to exit the ship."

She slapped his hand again. *Why is he getting ahead of her instructions?* She punched the Comm-link. "Captain Gadara to Control."

"Control, go ahead."

"Permission to exit the ship." She turned and glared at Conolly.

"Permission granted, Captain."

As Control opened the landing pad to the vastness of space, Conolly turned the ship around to face the opening, then shoved the lever forward and sped out of the Concordance. They barely slipped through the opening.

"Whoa!" She reached for the Nav-U-Comm.

He glanced at her once they were out of the ship's range.

She had one hand on the Nav-U-Comm, and the other, clutched the arm rest. "What in the Vaedran hell do you think you're doing?" Her anger boiled up inside her.

"Oh, man, this feels great! Wahoo!" He threw his head back as he yelled. "What a rush!" He glanced at her and smiled.

She crossed her arms and gave him the 'you've pissed me off' look.

"Didn't you enjoy that?"

"I used to." She mumbled, trying to put the feelings behind her. Conolly managed to bring them back in his reckless demeanor.

"What happened to you?" he said softly.

She looked forward. She couldn't let him see into her heart. "I had a mate, once upon a time. We kept it a secret because we were in the same unit." The memories came flooding back. "He thought he was a better pilot than I was and constantly challenged me." Her heart pounded in her chest as she finally stole a glance at Conolly.

He genuinely looked concerned. She focused her attention back to the expanse of space.

"I finally said, 'prove it.' That's all he needed. We flew over the desert on Vestra Major. I'd flown it many times as a child, but it was his first time." The memory was vivid now and she continued. "We flew low over the Gershon Straights, but when we got to the ridge, he didn't pull up fast enough, and hit the rock wall. I watched it happen." She wiped at her eyes. "I flew back over the spot, but his ship exploded. There was nothing left of him or the ship."

Conolly touched her shoulder. The warmth of his touch surprised her. She took a deep breath, still facing forward.

"I couldn't fly after that. I had nightmares. It took a long time to get over it."

"I know how you feel." He removed his hand from her shoulder.

She turned and glared at him. "Do you? Have you ever lost a mate or someone you loved, but couldn't tell anyone about it?"

"Yes. I did."

His sincerity gave her pause.

"All these pilots you're training are inexperienced, aren't they?"

"Of course! They wouldn't be taking my class if they knew how to fly."

"Well, I'm a test pilot. I've flown all kinds of planes, jets, and rockets. Hell, I've even flown alien space craft you fly with your mind." He touched the side of his head.

Her eyes widened. *Alien space craft you fly with your mind? Where has she heard that before?*

"I fly these different things to test them, to see how far we can push them, and see what they are really capable of doing, you know? So other pilots can do things in emergencies the ships weren't known to do."

He paused, then continued softly. "My best friend and I were both test pilots. I'm a better pilot, but he challenged me as well. We were testing a couple jets, but his crashed. I radioed it in. When I landed, they said he didn't make it. Then they proceeded to talk me into a secret test program for flying alien space ships and experimental planes. The catch was, that I would be listed as killed in the crash as well, so we both no longer existed. My sister was engaged to him."

She didn't understand. "What is engaged?"

"That's where you promise to take someone as a mate. My sister lost both of us that day. I lost my best friend, my sister and parents, all because I was young and stupid."

She touched his shoulder. "I'm sorry for your loss."

He shrugged. "Let's see what this baby can do."

He turned the ship upside down, did flips, spins, changed directions, stalled out and re-started the ship, plus a couple things she didn't know it could do.

"I think you've done enough for today," she said. "We need to find the Concordance."

"Did you have fun?"

She glanced at him. "Yes, but don't tell anyone." He smiled at her and she found herself smiling back.

He pushed some buttons on the Nav-U-Comm to lock onto the Concordance.

"You need to remember to always wear your helmet,

especially if you are testing ships in our system." She reached up above his head and opened a compartment. Then she reached up above her head and pulled hers out. She put her helmet on and watched him do the same.

"Why do we need to do this?"

"If you are wearing your helmet, it will save your life in case of an accident." She showed him the lever to push. "This will fit to your shoulders and give you enough oxygen to live an additional fifteen minutes." She pulled off the helmet and put it away. She watched him do the same.

"Good to know." He leaned closer. "I'll get us back safe and sound."

As they pulled up to the back of the Concordance, he called in to request permission to enter the ship.

"So, how did I do?"

"I can't pass you until you do ground and water landings. We can't do those until we reach Vestra Major."

"So are we doing the wing ship next?"

"No. My class is doing the transporters next, and you'll be joining them. They've already read the manual. Tomorrow is testing, then simulator work, and you're behind."

"Can I start the manual today, so I can catch up?" He looked hopeful.

"I'll think about it."

"When will you let me know?"

"After our mid-day meal. I'm starving."

He pulled into the Concordance and landed the wedge on the first try. He seemed as if he was 'one with the ship.' That was rare for someone just learning. She had to remember he wasn't a beginner, but an experienced pilot. She had thought he knew little about flying, or maybe she just assumed that. She would have words with the admiral. Maybe he didn't know either.

Once the all-clear was sounded, she grabbed Conolly's arm before he opened the hatch on the ship.

"Not a word about my story to anyone, you got that?"

He leaned toward her. Too close for comfort. "I'll keep your secret, Gadara, if you keep mine."

❄   *9*   ❄

"Follow me to the Sim Room and I'll give you the manual on transporters," Captain Gadara said.

"Yes, Captain Gadara." Conolly hoped she hadn't caught his latest slip-up where he used her name and not her title. He felt they had shared something so deep, that maybe they were getting a little personal. At least, he hoped so.

She opened the cabinet behind her desk and pulled out the Comm-Pad and pulled up the manual on transporters.

"Here you go. If you finish it early enough tomorrow, you can join the class in sim work."

"Captain Gadara," he began.

"Yes?"

"Do you think this is really necessary, I mean, since I'm an experienced pilot?"

"You are a reckless pilot and I think you need this manual more than anyone else in my unit."

"Ouch!" He gave her a salute and left. He wasn't reckless, but he did take chances, pushing the envelope. That was part of the job, wasn't it? To take the chances so other pilots would know if their planes could be pushed beyond what was known?

As he passed the Ancillary and laundry facilities, he realized he had to wash his uniform and his only unicrin that Eno gave him to use. He headed to his quarters to get his Air Force uniform to wash first, then he'd have to change and wash the one he wore. While he waited for his laundry, he would read the damn Comm-Pad.

Once he got to his quarters, Eno was just leaving.

"Hey, Eno, I need to do my laundry, but I don't have any money on me. Will they do credit cards?"

"Laundry? Hey, I'll take care of that if you do mine as well."

"Sure, no problem. I'll be reading this manual while I wait." He displayed the Comm- pad.

"Ugh. I hated that manual." Eno opened the door and gathered his dirty clothes, while he grabbed his own laundry bag.

Eno handed him a card. "Take this. It will let you use the laundry facilities."

Minutes later, he entered the Ancillary. The clerk stood by a register of sorts. "Do you have laundry soap?"

"Of course, over there." She pointed down an aisle. He found what he was looking for and returned to the front of the store.

"Do you have a razor, too?"

"What's a razor?"

"You know, for shaving." He rubbed his chin.

The woman gave him a blank look.

"Don't you people shave?"

"What is shave?"

Wow. If they didn't shave, they wouldn't know what a

razor was. "Uh, never mind." He handed her Eno's card and she rang up his soap.

He walked down the hall to the laundry facilities. After studying the instructions on the strange-looking machine, he had his Air Force uniform, socks, skivvies and t-shirt washing while he sat back and powered up the Comm-Pad. He started reading the manual on the device.

The transporters required two pilots because there was too much going on simultaneously for one to do the job. But since he was learning this ship, he had to know how to do all of it. He had read for some time when he realized the machine had stopped. He studied the instructions again and realized the machine did more than wash, but it had to be programmed for the drying cycle. He'd have to wait until he had something dry to wear before putting in his unicrin, along with Eno's stuff.

He finally figured out the procedure and returned to his reading. It was another hour before he realized the machine had stopped again. He set the Comm-Pad down on his seat, and headed to the machine. The clothes were dry. He rubbed his forehead again, feeling the headache return.

He found a cleansing unit in the laundry and went inside to change. He put on his skivvies and pants. Stepping out of the cleansing unit, he dropped his shoes beside his seat and hung up his uniform shirt on the back of it. He folded his t-shirt, sitting on the seat next to his, and proceeded to wash all the unicrins. He couldn't believe they wore boots without socks around here. He sat down and continued reading for some time when he heard voices in the room. He looked up and two young women, dressed in light gray unicrins, stared at him and whispered to each other.

"Is something wrong?" he asked.

The two women ran out of the room. How odd. He

checked on his unicrins and reprogrammed them into the dryer mode.

When he returned to his seat, Gadara had just picked up his Comm-Pad.

"Don't lose my spot!"

She glanced at the device and hit the bookmark to pause the pages. "Here you go." She handed him the Comm-Pad. Her eyes bore into his as her fingers brushed his in the exchange.

"I'm impressed you read so much all ready."

"You're impressed with my reading skills but not my piloting skills?"

She glanced away. "I meant, you don't follow directions."

"That's a hell of a lot different than being reckless, don't you think?"

She moved to an empty machine and dropped the contents of her laundry bag into it. She moved gracefully around the machine. He realized he could see the outline of her naked flesh beneath the almost sheer fabric of her white unicrin.

"You know, you Vaedrans really need to re-evaluate your style of unicrin."

"Why do you say that?" She turned to face him.

"Because I can see through your unicrin."

"And do you not like what you see?"

He swallowed hard before answering. "Hell, yeah, but I wouldn't want everyone else to see you like that."

"You would have us wear something like that?" She pointed to his uniform pants.

"At least I'm covered."

"Not from where I stand." She pointed to his chest and crossed her arms, accentuating her full breasts. He knew if he lowered his gaze, he wouldn't be able to concentrate on the manual anymore.

"My shirt was just washed. I'm trying to keep it from getting wrinkled. I wear my t-shirt under it." He stood to confront her.

She stared at his bare chest. "Vaedrans don't have chest hair."

He glanced down at the sparse black hairs on his chest. "They don't?" That might be why the two young women whispered about him. He glanced up and Gadara had moved very close.

"May I?" His gaze caught hers, as she reached her hand toward his chest.

Her touch seared him. His heart pounded, as she played with the hairs on his chest. "Very soft."

Her glance moved to his arms. "You have arm hair as well?"

"We have hair in other places, too." He caught her gaze, her hand still resting on his chest. "I'd be glad to so you in more private quarters."

She removed her hand and gave him a half smile. "I'll be right back."

He watched her walk out of the laundry facilities, then closed his eyes momentarily. What just happened? He hadn't noticed how sheer her unicrin was, because he hadn't looked at her like that before. He had women in the past, before he was written off, but none affected him like this, even briefly.

He sat down and awakened the Comm-Pad, trying to concentrate on what he needed to know about flying the transporters. It was difficult and he didn't get far when she re-entered the room with two bottles in her hands.

"Here." She offered him one of the bottles.

"Uh, thanks. I think." This was an odd gesture from his superior officer. He watched her take a sip, then followed suit.

It tasted like an ale. "Not bad. You would like what we have on Earth."

"You have ale on Earth?"

"Ale, beer, moonshine, liquor, you name it, we got it." He took another sip. He couldn't remember the last time he had a beer. This was definitely not helping him study, especially since each sip tasted better than the last.

She moved to sit next to him, so he pulled his t-shirt off the chair and held it in his lap, the Comm-Pad on top.

"I'm sorry for insulting your pilot skills. I'm not used to working with someone of your…caliber."

He took a sip while glancing at her. "You're not so bad yourself. You just need to loosen up a bit. You know, enjoy life more."

"I do!"

"You do, what?"

"Enjoy life."

"You don't act like it. You don't even act as if you enjoy flying."

"I used to love it." She closed her eyes. A tear ran down her check. He leaned over and reached his finger to her face, catching the tear. She opened her eyes and their gazes met. He wanted to kiss her. She needed to be kissed. He leaned closer.

"You can start again, you know." He practically kissed her while speaking to her.

"Start what?" She didn't flinch from his nearness.

"Enjoying life. Tomorrow, take some chances. Let yourself go."

Then the buzzer went off for the dryer. He pulled back a little and watched her lick her lips. He sat back in his seat and took a long drink of his ale, finishing it off. That kiss could have landed him in the brig.

"Well, my laundry is done. Thanks for the ale, Captain Gadara." He gathered his things and headed for his quarters. There was no way he could study with her around.

Once he was back in his room, he put up his uniform shirt and t-shirt and folded his unicrin. Then he folded Eno's unicrins, putting them on his shelf. When he found his socks, he realized he forgot his shoes.

The door buzzer sounded. When he answered it, Gadara stood before him. She pushed him back and stepped inside, letting the door hiss closed.

"You forgot something." She dropped his shoes near the bed and pushed him against the wall of the cleansing unit. She reached behind his head and pulled him toward her, kissing him tenderly on the mouth.

He pulled her tight against his body, his groin reacting immediately, and returned the kiss, only with more passion than he anticipated. And she returned her own passionate kiss.

When she pulled away, she spoke mere inches from his lips. "Not a word of this to anyone." She glared at him.

"You keep saying that. Do you think I want to go back to the brig?"

She kissed him tenderly and walked out as if nothing happened.

He climbed up on his bunk with the Comm-Pad. "If only you were Gadara," he said to the device. "I'd like to open her up and read her pages."

He studied the manual the rest of the night, skipping the evening meal, up until Eno turned out the light.

～

Gadara punched her pillow. What had she been thinking? She had already broken every rule she set for herself concerning men. Thoughts of Conolly without a shirt made her think about touching him more. And she definitely wanted to take him up on his invitation to see hair in other places.

She settled for remembering how his arms felt around her when he kissed her. She hadn't had that kind of touch in so long and she wanted more of it. But the kiss was different. It felt more passionate than she had ever experienced with her mate, Dax.

❧ 10 ❧

Sometime in the middle of the night, Eno heard Conolly stir in his bed. He rolled over, thinking Conolly would use the cleansing compartment, but when the light from the hallway shined into the room, Eno sat up.

"Conolly. Where are you going?"

Conolly stepped out into the hall, wearing his military pants from Earth, and headed toward the stairs.

Eno threw off his covers and grabbed his unicrin. He had the pants on and headed into the hallway, pulling on the sleeves.

"Conolly?" He checked the stairs, but didn't see Conolly in either direction. It was after curfew. What was Conolly up to? He had warned him about breaking curfew. He headed back to his room and checked his chrono. It was an hour before his alarm would go off. He decided Conolly was on his own. He would try to get another hour's sleep before facing the day. This would have to be part of his report to the admiral.

He slipped into the empty laundry room and the lights popped on at his movement. This would work. He powered up the Comm-Pad to where he left off last night and continued to read. He didn't have much left and he wanted to do the sim work with the class. If only he could get rid of this headache. He rubbed his temples, then above his brows, but the pain persisted.

He finished the book just as his alarm went off on his watch. Just in time to get back to the room and change for the day. He definitely wanted breakfast this morning since he missed dinner the night before.

Just as his door hissed open, he saw Eno exiting the cleansing compartment.

"Where have you been?" Eno asked.

"I went to the laundry room and finished this damn manual. We have sim practice today and I didn't want to be behind."

"Well, that's dedication. You could have been caught after curfew."

"Oh, yeah. I forgot about that." He had been worried about going to the brig for kissing Gadara, but he had forgotten the curfew. "That was close. Thanks for the reminder."

He quickly jumped in the shower and got dressed so he and Eno could head to breakfast together.

"I really appreciate all your help, Eno. Here's your card for the laundry. I forgot to give it back yesterday."

"No problem. I hate doing laundry."

"You know what I realized yesterday?"

"What's that?"

"You can see through the white unicrins."

"Yeah. We've complained about it over the years, but no one has changed anything about it."

The two of them entered the eating hall, grabbed some food, and found a table.

"I'm anxious to get through the sim work today," Conolly said. He took a bite of his eggs.

"Why is that?"

"So we can fly tomorrow."

"You are going through this class pretty fast, aren't you?" Eno sipped his drink.

"Yes. I didn't want to hold Gadara up from her lessons." He stuffed a piece of bread into his mouth. "Everyone else is about finished and I wanted to get done before we arrive in Vestra Major."

"Gadara now, is it? Are you two on a first name basis?"

"No." He wished they were. "We talk about our superior officers on Earth by using their last names at times, but I don't know her last name."

"We don't really have last names here. We use our parents' name. I'm Eno ni Esrith, which means Eno, son of Esrith." Eno took a bite of his eggs.

"Well, I'm Torin Conolly. Conolly is my father's last name so I have a first and last name."

"Torin?"

"Yes, it's Irish. We're of Irish decent."

"Is that a place on Earth?"

He nodded while he ate. "Well, I'm an American, from the United States of America. My ancestors came from Ireland and moved to America. So people from Ireland are Irish."

"That's very confusing. Our home planet is Vestra Major. Everyone came from there. When we colonized the planets, every race got their own planet. Our new home planet is

Chroma. If you see anyone here with blond hair and blue eyes, we are Chromian. There are quite a few of us on this ship."

"Chromian is a race?"

"Yes. There's Tarsian from Tarsius, Vestrian from Vestra Minor, Plexan from Plexus, Persians from Persus, Atrians from Atria, and the Caucus people like Captain Gadara and Tremol come from Vestra Major. Plumaris is our penal colony. Only criminals live there under heavy guard."

"Will this be on a test?"

"No." Eno laughed. "I just thought I'd fill you in on our people." Eno glanced at his watch. "Well, I've got a meeting at 0930 this morning. When does your class start?"

He glanced at his own watch. It was 0850. "I think in ten minutes. I've got to get the Comm-Pad and head to class."

He rushed out of the eating hall and back to his room.

The device was on his bunk. He grabbed it and headed to the Sim Room. After sharing that steamy kiss with Gadara, something told him the class would never be the same.

Gadara finished her meal and headed for the Sim Room to get things set up for class. She was actually looking forward to class today. The whole group would be together. She doubted Conolly would have finished the manual by now, so he would work on that while the others took their tests. Only she didn't have seven simulators, she had six. Hers was a monitor to watch how the others were doing. And where was she going to put Conolly? Her desk was the only thing left.

She would have to improvise. She could let him sit at her desk to read. She pulled open the closet. She had only six

Comm-Pads set up for the test. She pulled her personal Comm-Pad out and programmed it for the test, just in case.

Finally, everything was ready. She would get the class started, then slip out to her daily staff meeting with the admiral.

The admiral. She needed to tell him what Conolly told her, but that would betray his secret. Then he could betray her. He could reveal what had transpired between them. She would lose her commission and everything she wanted in her career.

Just then, the door hissed open and a couple of her students came in. "Good morning boys! Hope you studied well for the test."

"Yes, Captain Gadara," one of them said. The two took their regular seats at the simulators.

The simulators! She had to re-program one of them since Conolly had used it. She moved to the front and checked it, making sure it was set to transporter mode. She decided to check all of them, just to make sure. As she checked the sims, another couple students entered. When she finished the last one, Conolly stood before her, the Comm-Pad in his hand.

"Ah, Conolly. Did you need more time to read the manual?"

"No, Captain Gadara. I finished it." He smiled as he handed the Comm-Pad to her.

"You did?"

"Yes, Captain, I did."

She glanced around the room and realized everyone was seated but Conolly.

"Class, I'd like you to meet Torin Conolly, from Earth. He will be training with you for the duration of our trip."

"Conolly, come with me." She walked to the back of the room. "You'll be using my desk since we have no more simulators available." He sat down and watched her as she moved to the cabinet. She handed him her Comm-Pad and then retrieved the other six. After handing them out to everyone, she checked her chrono.

"All right, turn on the Comm-Pads."

Conolly did as he was told.

She gave the signal for them to begin. She stood in the back by the door and waited to make sure everyone was able to work without any more questions, then she slipped out to go to the meeting.

She was still surprised to find he finished reading the manual so fast. He didn't have a whole day like the last manual and this one was longer. She would definitely recommend that these classes went faster than she had been doing them in the past. Then she realized this was the last time she would be teaching these classes. A sad feeling ran through her.

The admiral went over some things about the day and then asked the question she dreaded.

"Do you have anything to report, Captain Gadara?"

"I have a question, Admiral. What alien group has ships that are flown with the mind?"

"I would have to do more research on that, Captain Gadara, but there is only one that I know of right now and that is the greys."

"The greys?" another officer asked.

"Yes. I'll get back to the rest of you on that tomorrow," the admiral said.

As the group got up to leave, the admiral put his hand on her shoulder.

"A word with you, Captain," he said.

She held her breath. What would she say? She couldn't lie to him but she didn't want to betray Conolly.

Once the room cleared out, she stood before him. "Yes, Admiral?"

"Where did you hear of this ship?"

"I heard about it, Admiral, but I promised not to reveal any more information."

"Why is that?" He eyed her intently.

"It's confidential, sir." She hoped that would be enough for him.

"You wouldn't be holding back any information now, would you?"

"All I will say, Admiral, is that someone on this ship has flown that type of ship on Earth."

"Hmmm. That will be all, Captain."

She raced back to the Sim Room. Why did she even bring the matter up? It happened in the past. No one needed to know about it. It doesn't affect them. Besides, there weren't very many people here from Earth, now, were there? Then she remembered all the dignitaries. Of course! There were at least twenty-three other people plus Keely and Adam. Some of the dignitaries were military people. If only the admiral would believe that.

When she entered the room, everyone was still taking the test but Conolly. He sat in her seat, his left arm propping up his head, drumming his right fingers on the desk.

"Are you having a problem, Conolly?" she whispered.

"No, Captain Gadara. I'm finished," he whispered back. He handed her the Comm-Pad. She took the device and went through his answers. After a few minutes, she realized he hadn't missed any this time, either.

She squatted beside the seat. "I don't have enough simulators for you to work on." She whispered again.

"Why don't we just go to the transporters and fly them?" he whispered back with a smile.

"Nice try." She patted his leg, then stood up.

One of her other students came up to her with his Comm-Pad.

"Are you finished?"

"Yes, Captain Gadara." He handed it to her.

"You can have a ten-minute break and then work on the simulator."

She checked his answers as well. He had missed two, but he was still eligible to do simulator work. She picked up her own Comm-Pad and entered his grade in her records. She felt heat coming from behind her and turned into Conolly. He was inches away from her.

"Yes?"

"Am I in that device?"

"No, actually. You aren't in the Vaedran Military, so I don't need to put you in here."

Two more students brought up their Comm-Pads.

"You both can have a ten-minute break before doing simulator work."

"What about me?" Conolly asked.

"What about you?"

"Don't I get a ten-minute break?"

"Yes, of course. I'm sorry." She had grown fond of his nearness and had forgotten he was behind her.

"I forgive you," he whispered in her ear. His breath, coupled with his closeness, sent shivers down her spine.

She shook off the feelings as she went over the other

Comm-Pads. By the time she finished checking and recording grades, the first student returned.

She got him started on the simulator. Then, one by one, they all returned but Conolly. The simulators would take a couple hours at the least, if they were fast. If not, it could take up to four. She would end up stopping the class for them to take a mid-day meal break.

She checked her chrono. It had been almost twenty minutes. She went out into the hall to look for Conolly. Where was he?

When she turned the corner, she saw him standing with the admiral, Tremol, and Keely in the hall.

11

Her heart pounded in her chest. What had she done? Now he could betray her secrets. She would lose her commission in the Star Force.

"Captain Gadara. Just the person we need to speak to." The admiral gestured for her to join them.

She walked toward the group. Conolly eyed her but she couldn't read his expression.

"Yes, Admiral?"

"I asked Keely and Tremol what they knew of the alien population on Earth."

Interesting way to put it. "Yes, Admiral?"

"It seems the shadow government has kept a lot of secrets from even the Secret Service."

"I'm with the Secret Service, Captain Gadara," Keely began. "Until I met Tremol, I didn't know we had an alien population on Earth. There were a lot of conspiracy theories out there, but it turns out most of them were true after all. Even my parents had been visited by the greys and had been abducted. The greys implanted some strange pieces of alien technology into their bodies."

"I've heard of this treatment by the greys." It was in her military training years ago.

"If it wasn't for Tremol and Conn, my parents would still be in pain from these devices." Keely put her arm around Tremol when she spoke. And Tremol reciprocated. It was a gesture Gadara had always wanted done to her by her mate, but it never happened. She blinked the thought away.

"Conolly here has volunteered to be scanned for any alien devices," the admiral said.

She blinked. "I'm sorry. I don't understand."

"I told Keely that I'd been having headaches. I didn't know if your people had them, so I told her. I knew she would understand," Conolly said.

"I told Mr. Conolly that my mother had headaches and it turned out she had an alien implant in her brain."

"I offered to have Conn in the Med Facilities scan him for any implants and he volunteered," the admiral said. "Shall we?" He gestured for them to follow.

She glanced at her chrono. Her class would be busy for a while. She followed the group to the Med Facilities.

Once inside, Conn ushered them to the scan room.

"Put this on," she said. Conn handed Conolly a small coverup.

"That's all I get? On Earth, we have a little more than this to cover up with." Conolly said.

Conn showed him where to change. "The rest of you don't need to be here, but if you must, you can wait over there." She pointed to an area about twenty feet away.

The admiral's communicator went off. "I'll be right there," he said, answering it. "You can give me a report later, Captain." He left the Med Facilities.

Conolly stepped out of the cleansing compartment with the tiniest piece of cloth she had ever seen. He was well built and muscular all over. She had already had the opportunity to see his upper body with the dark chest hairs that led down past the tiny cloth. But now, she noticed his legs had hair on them as well. Not a lot, but it was noticeable.

Conn showed him to the table and he sat down. "Oh, that's cold," he said.

Gadara moved to where Keely and Tremol stood. She watched as Conn had him lie down and ran the scanner over his body, starting at the head.

On the large screen, she could see an object up past his nose. As the scanner continued, she could see another object in his right thigh.

Keely leaned close and whispered. "My parents had one device in each of them. Looks like he's got two."

She knew Conn had experience removing these items, plus, she was a healer. Conolly would be in good hands.

"I can remove these now, if you want? I don't have any scheduled procedures today." Conn spoke to Conolly.

"Is this a dangerous procedure?" Conolly asked.

"No. But I'll have to keep you for observation the rest of the day."

She walked over to the table, where Conolly sat up.

"Captain, will this interfere in my classwork today?"

"You know I don't have enough simulators, so no, you're free to go through with it, if you want."

"Conn, will I be able to fly tomorrow?" he asked.

"I don't see why not."

"Now wait a minute. I won't let you fly unless you go through the simulator first."

"But you just said you didn't have enough. I can do this," he said.

"When will you have time for the simulator?" She asked.

"Maybe I can work on the simulator while I'm being observed?"

"I think we can arrange that," Conn said.

Why did she feel as if someone else was running her training program? "I'll think about it," she said.

Conn moved around the table and strapped Conolly down. She had her assistant help her prepare the room for the procedure.

"I'm giving you something that will help you sleep so we can remove these devices," Conn said. She injected him with the medication. "It will take a few minutes to kick in."

"I will be back when the procedure is over," Gadara said to Conolly.

"Don't go," Conolly pleaded.

"What?"

"Please?"

His eyes pleaded with her. He looked helpless, strapped to the table. "Whoa! This stuff feels like I just guzzled a Long Island Ice Tea," he said.

She glanced over at Keely, who had moved closer to the table. "That's a drink about as potent as the Detonator," Keely said.

"My head is spinning. No, the room is spinning," Conolly said. He smiled at her.

Tremol glanced at Conolly. "He looks pretty happy to me."

Conn moved closer. "It won't be long now."

"Can I have a minute alone with the Captain?" Conolly asked.

She was surprised at his request and shrugged her shoulders.

"Come along." Conn gestured for Keely and Tremol to leave with her.

"What is it, Conolly?" She leaned a little closer.

His eyelids were drooping as if he was about to fall asleep.

"I wanted you to be the last thing I tasted before I am out and the first thing I see when I open my eyes."

"What do you mean?" Her heart pounded in her chest.

"I'd love for you to kiss me like you did the other night."

She glanced around, but no one else was in the room. She leaned close and gave him a tender kiss. He was conscious enough to return it and then he was out. She tenderly touched the side of his face. It felt prickly, but he looked handsome in his sleep.

She left the area and found Conn and the others outside the door. "He's out. He wants me to be there when he awakens."

"I can alert you on your communicator, Captain."

"Thank you, Conn. That would be nice."

"Can you notify us as well?" Keely asked.

"Yes."

They went separate ways. She had a class to check on, but her lips still burned from his kiss. It wasn't nearly as passionate as the night before, but it would sustain her. She hoped Conolly enjoyed it as much as she did.

The class was nearly done with the first three scenarios in the flight simulator when she decided to give them a meal break. They could pause their simulators and pick up where they left off.

As they filed out of the room, one of her students asked, "Where's the new pilot?"

"He's having a procedure done in the Med Facilities as we speak. Why?"

"I was just wondering how we were all going to get our flight time in tomorrow."

"We have enough ships for the whole class."

"Yes, but he hasn't done his sim work. Won't he be behind?"

"He's managed to read the manual in one day, take the test and do the simulator work and fly in two days for the wedge ship. I think he'll manage somehow." Just then, she realized she would help make it happen so he could fly with the class.

Before she could head to the eating hall herself, her communicator went off. "I'll be right there, Conn. Thank you."

She headed for the Med Facilities and got there just in time for Conolly to open his eyes. She couldn't help but smile at his sleepy face. She wouldn't mind seeing that in the mornings.

She touched the side of his face like before.

"What a beautiful sight," he said.

"Thank you. I hope you're feeling better."

"Well, when this hangover is gone, I should feel just fine.

She noticed he wasn't strapped down anymore. "Has Conn brought you anything to eat?"

He glanced around. "I don't see any food."

"She might want you to wait a while. I was heading to the eating hall if you want me to pick something up for you?"

He reached for her arm. "I'm sorry I've caused so much trouble. I…flying is everything to me. I don't know what I'd do if I couldn't fly."

"You've actually been quite entertaining," she said.

"I have? How?"

"I've never seen such dedication before."

"But what about my flying?"

"You're good, Conolly. Really good, but I just can't trust you alone."

"Why not?"

"You take too many chances. Those ships are my responsibility and so are the pilots."

"I get it. You want me to fly like a newbie."

"Could you?"

"It would be boring as hell, but for you, Captain, I'd do anything."

❄   I 2   ❄

After Conn released Conolly to her, she insisted he put his clothes back on before she pushed him in the hover chair. His right leg was propped up straight as she moved him to the Sim Room.

"Let me know if you are uncomfortable and I'll get you back to the Med Facilities."

"This is fine, Captain. I really appreciate you letting me catch up like this."

"If I didn't do this, I don't know what I'd do with you tomorrow when the rest of us will be flying."

She parked him in the back at the last row of simulators. The rest of the class had finished and were off for the remainder of the night. They were all to meet at 1030 on the flight deck.

"You're all set. You'll have to do this at a slight angle since your leg is in the way."

"I'll figure it out, Captain. Thanks." He winked at her.

"I promised the admiral I'd fill him in on your progress, so you're on your own for a little while. I'll come back and check on you." She patted his shoulder and left.

He wore his Earthen military clothes since the procedure. Before that, he had on his flight suit from the Vaedran Military. He would be better off wearing the Vaedran clothes when flying their ships. It would look better with the other pilots, otherwise he would stand out.

She was kidding herself. He did stand out, even in their unicrin. He was far better looking than any of her students and older, closer to her own age. And he was taller than all her students. In fact, he and Eno were the tallest men on the ship.

She headed to the one place she knew the admiral would be after the evening meal. The Officers Lounge.

"Hello, Captain Gadara. Are you here on official business?" the admiral asked. He sat at the bar and pulled a seat out for her. "A Detonator for the captain, please," he said to the barkeep.

"That depends on my report. Did you want it officially or as a curiosity?"

"I'm always curious, Gadara. How's your class going?"

"Everyone seems to be doing fine. Tomorrow we fly the transporters."

"Didn't you already do those?"

"I flew the transporters with one co-pilot in the Nav-U-Comm and the rest as guests. They took turns co-piloting and then piloting when we were back on Earth. We were able to do some landings as well. They had read the manuals, they just hadn't taken the test until this morning and the sim work this afternoon. Tomorrow, we'll review the pre-flight and I'll send two out in each ship. They need the flight time for experience."

"What about Conolly?" he asked.

"I didn't know the extent of his knowledge as a pilot so I went through everything as if I was teaching a newbie."

"But he was a test pilot."

"Yes, but I didn't realize how good he was."

"So he's the one who flew the alien craft?"

Her eyes widened. The admiral was no fool. "Admiral, please don't mention that I said anything to you about that. I…confided some things to him and if he finds out I broke his trust, well, I just don't want to do that."

"Your secrets are safe, Gadara. But now that the alien devices have been removed, he can't be controlled by them."

"Do you think that's why he was here?"

"He was sent by either the greys or the shadow government the President warned me about."

The barkeep brought her Detonator and sat it down, then glanced up at the entrance. She looked over her shoulder and saw a military man, wearing a similar unicrin as that of Conolly.

"General," the admiral said.

"Are Earthen Officers allowed in here?"

"Of course, come and join us." The admiral pulled out a seat on his other side. "This is Captain Gadara, our flight instructor. Gadara, this is General Thompson of the—"

"U.S. Army. Thanks, Admiral." The general reached across in front of the admiral and shook her hand. "I'm one of the Joint Chiefs of Staff for the President. We're all here, anxious to purchase some of your high-tech ships and equipment."

"Barkeep, bring the general a Detonator as well," the admiral said.

"I don't suppose we could get someone like the captain to come to Earth to train our pilots on how to fly these ships?"

Gadara choked on her drink. The admiral patted her back.

"You all right Gadara?"

She coughed out a yes.

"Did I say something to offend you, Captain?" the general asked.

She glanced at the admiral. "No. You surprised me. I was under the impression that Astronaut Torin Conolly was here to learn how to fly the ships to train others back on Earth."

The General choked on his drink. "Torin Conolly?"

"Yes, sir."

"Astronaut Torin Conolly was killed in a crash years ago, along with his co-pilot, while testing a new stealth jet. It was in all the news."

She glanced at the admiral and then the general. "Can you identify him if you see him?"

"I think so, but General Stevens, of the U.S. Air Force, would know him better. I think he was at the funeral. Why do you ask?"

"Because I've been training *him* to fly our ships."

❀ 13 ❀

She stood over Conolly while he finished up his sim work. "Do you know a General Thompson?"

He looked up at her. "No, I don't think so. What branch is he in?"

"Branch? I don't know what that means."

"Army, Navy, Air Force?"

"I believe he said Army." She crossed her arms.

"Why?"

"He said you were killed in a crash."

He touched her elbow, sending a flash of heat throughout her body. "Gadara, I told you they faked that so I could be in the secret test pilot program, remember? No one knows that I'm still alive. Not even my sister."

"It was strange, hearing that from someone else." Could it be as he said, everyone else believing the lie?

"I'm touched." He winked at her and caught her off guard again. Why did he keep doing that?

"Have you finished your sim work?" She needed to change the subject, feeling uncomfortable.

"Yes, Captain. Now, can you help me to my room?"

She grabbed the handles of his hover chair and pushed him to the people mover. "I hope you're on the lower bunk," she said.

"Actually, I'm on top."

She stopped in her tracks. "You aren't supposed to bend your leg just yet." She headed to the Med Facilities instead.

She found Conn. "Conolly will need a place to sleep tonight," she said.

"Oh. I'm sorry. We only have a few beds and they are in use tonight. Had I known, I wouldn't have scheduled the procedures."

"I understand." She turned Conolly around and headed toward her room.

"Where are we going?"

"My place." Once she arrived at her room, she guided the hover chair through the doorway.

"I'm impressed Captain. Your room is more homey than Eno's."

"I outrank him." It was true, but she also managed to get a nice easy chair in her room as well.

"Stay here," she said. She pulled the cover and sheet back on her bed. She could easily sleep on top since he was in no condition to climb up.

"Did you need to use the cleansing compartment?"

He glanced at her, then the cleansing unit. "Yes. Just get me through the door, I'll take it from there."

She waited for him outside the door. This would be awkward, to say the least, since she usually slept in the nude. She searched through her drawers for something she could wear for sleeping in and pulled out a shim. She wore it when she was off duty and just stayed in her quarters.

When he came out, he was wearing only a small pair of pants, sitting in the hover chair.

"What are those?" She couldn't help stare at his bare legs and muscular thighs.

"We call them skivvies or underwear."

"Underwear?"

"Yes, you wear them under your clothes."

"Why?"

"For comfort and some privacy. Don't you wear any?"

"Of course not."

"Why not?"

"We've never had anything like that."

"I know. I can see through your unicrin."

"If you don't like what you see—"

"But I do." He pushed himself up off the chair, balancing on his good leg, and wrapped his arm around her waist. He pulled her close. "You know, I feel I can use my leg," he said.

"Maybe tomorrow. Tonight, you need to rest."

"Yes Captain." But he didn't release her. Her pulse shot up and her heart beat faster. This was too close. She put her hand on his chest to push him away and he moved his hand from her waist to her neck and pulled her into a kiss. She was shocked at first until she realized she wanted this. She kissed him back, tenderly at first but her passion rose within her and she deepened the kiss. He had both arms around her, caressing her back, then holding her face with his hands.

She felt him pull her down to the bed and on top of him. He fidgeted with her unicrin and managed to release the shoulder magnets holding her top up. He rolled on top of her, his lips never breaking the bond. His hands roamed over her breasts, tenderly, gently. The explosion of sensory feelings caused her to moan.

She felt a tug on the bottom of her unicrin and sat up.

"This will never work."

"It's working so far."

"I'm wearing boots!" She leaned over the side of the bed to remove her shoes, then dropped the rest of her unicrin to the floor. He removed his skivvies. He reached his hand out to her and she took it. They picked up where they left off. She explored his alien body and he explored hers.

"What is this prickly stuff on your face?" she asked.

"It's hair. I don't have a razor."

"What is a razor?"

"Something we use on Earth to cut the hair off our faces. Otherwise, this will turn into a beard."

He kissed her neck, then rubbed his face against her skin. The sensations triggered a moan from her. He continued with the caressing, kissing, and exploring, until they came together in passionate ecstasy.

He enveloped her in his arms and for once, she felt complete. It had been so long since she had Dax, but she didn't remember it being like this. She wanted more. She hungered for the pleasure of his company.

She pulled the covers over both of them.

"You know, Gadara, no one has ever been this kind to me before." His words touched her and she froze.

He pulled her closer, cuddling with her from behind. She enjoyed his embrace, his arms around her middle, and she wrapped her arms over his. She drifted off to sleep.

Then a thought came to mind. What was she thinking? A man in her quarters! People would talk and assume they had mated. She knew nothing about him but let her passions run wild anyway. Did he know what this meant to her and her people?

She turned toward him and he kept his arms around her, pulling her close.

"I've never met anyone like you Gadara."

She felt comfortable in his arms, and yet she wondered how in the Vaedran hell was she going to get out of this mess.

Hours later, she tossed and turned.

"Can't sleep?" he asked.

"I've got a lot on my mind."

"Me, too. I'm wondering why I can't remember having those implants."

She stiffened. "You don't remember having any procedures done to you?"

"No. I don't remember being around any aliens, either. Other than you, of course."

"Conolly, on this ship, *you* are the alien."

"You're right. Sorry. But please call me Torin. At least when we're alone."

"Were you ever injured before?"

"No. I've always been in good health."

She propped herself up on her elbow to see his expression. "Do you have any lapse of memory?"

"No, that's why this seems so odd. I don't remember having headaches until recently, either."

"Didn't you say you flew alien ships with your mind?"

"Yes."

"Maybe there was something in that ship that affected you somehow."

"But that doesn't explain the implants. How did someone put those in me without me knowing about it?"

"By tampering with your memories."

He sat up. "What?"

"Someone tampered with your memories."

"How could they?"

"There are alien races out there that are capable of far more technology than we have in the Vaedra System."

"Are the greys more advanced?"

"In some ways, yes."

He pulled her toward him and wrapped his leg over her hip.

She touched his face with her hand. "If you want to fly tomorrow, go to sleep."

❧ 14 ❧

Gadara bolted up in her bed. She had to get Torin Conolly out of there without being seen. She glanced over at him. Damn, he looked good. She licked her lips. She had to stop thinking like that. She rolled out of bed and headed to the cleansing compartment. When she dried off, she realized Conolly's clothes were inside and now soaked.

She put on her unicrin and quickly fixed her hair. Before she headed out the door, Conolly woke up.

"Where are you going?"

"Stay there. I'll be right back." She pointed at him.

"Yes, Captain." He saluted her.

She slipped out into the hall and headed to Ancillary. She had to find him a unicrin and quick.

"Can I help you?" the clerk asked.

"Yes. I need a pilot's unicrin, but it's got to be for a tall man."

"I have one, but it's not tall."

"What have you got in tall?"

"An officer's unicrin."

"I'll take it." She paid her with credits and shoved the unicrin under her arm and headed down the hall.

"Captain Gadara?"

She stopped in her tracks at the sound of her name.

"Hello, Conn. What can I help you with?"

"I have something to show you. Come with me."

She followed Conn into the Med Facilities. Conn picked up a glass vessel holding two tiny objects.

"What is that?"

"These are the implants we pulled from Astronaut Conolly."

One was long and thin, the other was wider and fuller looking. While she watched, they started to vibrate.

"What's happening?"

"I believe someone on this ship is trying to control these two implants."

"Only they don't know they've been removed," she said.

"Exactly."

"How is this happening? I thought only the greys could control them through telepathy."

"Apparently, they've devised something that humans can use to control other humans."

"May I show this to the admiral?"

"Yes, of course."

She took the vessel and carried it back to her room with the unicrin. When she opened the door, Conolly stood naked inside the cleansing compartment, about to step out into the room.

"I hope you have something for me to wear?"

"Yes." She tossed him the unicrin. "Hurry and dress. I have something to show you."

"How did my clothes get wet?"

"You left them hanging inside the compartment and I didn't see them until I finished cleansing myself. I'm sorry."

"This is an officer's unicrin, isn't it?"

"Yes. They had nothing your size other than that."

"I guess I'll be doing laundry later today."

"You'll need to slip out and head back to your room before you're seen here."

"Are you trying to get rid of me?" He stood before her and pulled her into a kiss.

"Yes. I need to compose myself into a Captain once more." Her arms were around his neck.

"What were you going to show me?"

She pulled away and picked up the vessel. "See these implants?"

"Yes."

"I saw them vibrate a few minutes ago. Conn showed it to me."

"They aren't moving now."

"No. But what she said was, someone on this ship is trying to control them."

"You mean they are trying to control me?"

"Yes."

Just then, the two implants started vibrating again.

"Now all we have to do is figure out who it is."

"I'm taking this to the admiral and let him know Conn's findings."

"I'll head back to the room and see if Eno is up. After last night, I'm starving." He winked at her.

"Why do you do that?"

"Because I like you. A lot." He kissed her cheek and headed to the door.

"Wait!"

"What? Why?"

"I need to make sure the hall is clear." She stepped into the hall and looked both ways. "All clear."

He headed down the hall to the stairs. She watched him until he was gone.

Conolly ran his hand through his hair. He remembered his comb was in his back pocket of his Air Force uniform, still hanging in Gadara's quarters. His missed having pockets. The unicrins the Vaedrans wore had no pockets. And how was he going to explain himself to Eno? He hoped he hadn't missed him. He liked hanging out with him.

When he approached the doorway on Eno's quarters, it opened. Eno stood in the entrance, looking him over.

"Did I miss something? Have you been promoted?"

"No! I had an accident with my uniform and needed something to wear. Are you heading to breakfast? I mean, the morning meal?"

"Yes."

"Let's go, then. I'm starving."

Eno joined him in the hall and they headed for the stairs.

"Where were you last night? What happened to you?"

"It's a long story."

Once they were situated in the eating hall, Eno pushed his shoulder. "Start talking."

"My head was bothering me all the time I studied. I thought it was just stress but it got worse. When I ran into Keely and Tremol, I asked if she had any aspirin."

"What's that?"

"It's something we use on Earth for headaches."

Eno nodded. "We have things here for head pains as well."

"Well, while I was talking to her, the admiral walked up and the conversation turned to implants."

"Implants? Like in the greys?"

"So you know about those?"

"Yes. In the military, they go over all the alien races we know about and their military tactics."

"Well, the next thing I remember, I was being scanned for implants."

"And?"

He leaned forward to whisper. "I had two of them. One in my head and one in my leg."

"Did they remove them?"

"Shhh. Conn removed both of them. I was stuck in the Med Facilities for a while for observation." He shoved some eggs into his mouth. He realized he had been talking and not eating.

"So what about last night? Where were you?"

"Gadara, I mean Captain Gadara, set me up in the Sim Room so I could work on the simulators and fly today."

"All night?"

He couldn't expose her. Not even to Eno.

"I fell asleep."

"How did you get that unicrin?"

"Ancillary. No other unicrins my size." It was true. Sort of.

Eno finished his meal while he kept shoveling his down.

"What time are you flying today?"

He gulped the last of the coffee-flavored drink. "1030."

"I have a briefing this morning at 0930. All the ships are ready to go. I went over them yesterday. Which ships are you flying today?"

"Transporters."

"Remember, they don't handle like the wings or wedges."

"So I've been told. I'm supposed to fly like a newbie."

"Really?"

"Apparently the captain thinks I take too many risks."

❧ 15 ☙

There wasn't enough time to do laundry before flight time, so Conolly paced back and forth in Eno's quarters. Eno had already left for their briefing. He hoped Gadara wouldn't have to lie for him. He tried to contain his excitement. This is why he was here, to learn to fly these ships. But the truth was, he was really here to steal one of these ships and head back to Earth. The only ship that could do that was the transporter and not the wedge or wing ship he was to return in.

He tried to remember who gave him that order, but his mind was blank. Why those two ships? Whoever gave him the order may not have known those two ships couldn't handle the distance. Was the order tied to the implants? And when did he get those implants? Why couldn't he remember having the procedure done to him?

He glanced at his watch. He still had time before the flight training, so he headed to deck 7.

~

The admiral stood before the group. "We will be arriving at the jump point sometime this afternoon. You all know to be ready." He glanced around the room and stopped at Gadara. "Any questions?"

No one responded. "Dismissed."

She stood up and approached him. "A word with you, Admiral," she said.

The room cleared. She pulled the glass vessel out from under the cloth she had covered it with.

"What is that?"

"Conn gave this to me this morning. These are the implants taken from Astronaut Conolly."

The admiral held up the glass. The two implants vibrated again. "Is this what I think it is?" he asked.

"Yes," a male voice responded.

The Admiral and Gadara glanced in the direction of the voice. Eno approached them. "He was sent here to either sabotage our ships or to steal one."

"How do you know this?"

"It's a gut feeling. But the implants are a sign he is under alien control."

"Was under alien control," she corrected him.

"He didn't return to our quarters last night."

Her heart sank. Did he expose their mating last night?

"Did he tell you where he was?" the admiral asked.

"He said the captain set him up in the Sim Room and he fell asleep."

Both men glanced at her and her eyes widened. "I forgot all about him. I did set him up there. I didn't know what I was going to do with him while we were flying today, so I told him to do the sim work."

"Is he ready?" the admiral asked.

"I believe so. I have everyone paired up to fly the transporters. He will fly with me so I can keep an eye on him."

"Do you trust him?" the admiral asked.

She glanced at both men, concern on their faces.

"He can no longer be controlled by the implants. Maybe I can get some answers now." Her heart pounded when she realized she had forgotten her original mission.

"I will stand by if you need me, Captain." Eno said.

"Good. I appreciate that." She touched his arm. "We'll use Guardian Assist if it comes to that."

"You got it." Eno left the room.

"If it was an alien implant that brought him here, we have to find out who is behind it," the admiral said.

"I agree." She couldn't tell him what Conolly confided in her last night. Not yet.

Most of her class had arrived in the Sim Room, except Conolly. She glanced at her chrono. She couldn't wait much longer.

"We will begin. Let's head to deck 7."

"Aren't we waiting for the new pilot?" she heard someone ask.

"This is an unscheduled flight so you can get in more flight time maneuvers. You have your orders and we have a jump scheduled this afternoon. We must return before that." She led the group of trainees to deck 7. Where was Conolly? She couldn't hold the class up for him, but why was he late? He was always punctual before.

By the time they arrived at the flight deck, he stood there in his pilot's unicrin, looking over the deck at the ships below. How did he get that unicrin?

He saluted her. "Captain, sorry I'm late."

She saluted back and eyed him with curiosity. She pulled up her Comm-Pad and called out the team names and the ship they were to fly.

"Get to your ships."

"What about me, Captain?" Conolly asked.

"Come with me." She tensed her jaw. She hid her excitement at seeing him again. It had only been a couple of hours. How could she feel this way about him? She shook off the feeling and became Captain Gadara once more. She was strict and demanding. She didn't fawn over men.

Once inside her ship, she buckled up and prepared for pre-flight. She glanced over at Conolly and he had done the same.

"Well?" she said.

He looked at her. "Am I the pilot or co-pilot today?"

"Today, you are the pilot. Make me proud."

He smiled the most gorgeous smile she had seen on him. "Glad to, Captain." Then he winked.

She hid her smile from him. While Conolly was doing his checklist, she put her headset on to listen to each of her pilots at their Nav-U-Comms. She had to be attentive to all of them and still keep her mind on her own ship. This was a teaching ship. She would be giving this up at the end of her training program. She took a deep breath to clear the sadness that tried to break the moment.

One by one, she listened as each pilot requested permission to exit the Concordance. Finally, it was their turn.

"Conolly to Control."

"Control, go ahead."

"Request permission to exit the ship."

"Permission granted."

Carefully, Conolly moved the ship out from its berth and into space.

"How was that? Newbie enough for you?"

"Very good." She reached the Comm-link and contacted each ship simultaneously. "Your coordinates are locked in your database. Proceed to your destination. Once you arrive there, switch positions from pilot to co-pilot, and the other takes over to return you to this location."

"Copy that," each one reported.

She motioned for Conolly to hold position, as she watched each ship take off in different directions.

"Now it's your turn."

He searched his database for his location.

"Got it!"

"When did you have time to change unicrins?" Gadara asked.

"After the morning meal with Eno. I didn't want to stand out."

"Too late for that, Conolly."

"Please call me Torin when we are alone."

"Torin, did Eno ask about where you were last night?"

"I told him I fell asleep in the Sim Room."

"He didn't press for more information?"

"No, thank God. I didn't want to get you in trouble."

"You would be the one in trouble."

"How so?"

"Fraternizing with a superior officer. But since you aren't Vaedran Military, it could be overlooked."

"What happens now?" Torin asked.

"What do you mean?"

"With us? Do we pretend this didn't happen, or do we continue with our relationship and see where it goes?"

What could she say? They were mated for life, but did he understand that? "What do you know of Vaedran culture?"

"Not much. Why?"

"What happens on Earth if you mate with someone?"

"You mean, have sex?"

"Is that what you call it?"

"Well, there are several names for it, but having sex is sex."

"What did you want to happen?" she asked, preparing her heart for the worst.

"I want to continue our relationship." He reached out and caressed her cheek.

She wanted more of that, but she wanted to know that he was hers alone and she didn't want to hide the fact that they were mates, like she did with Dax.

Out of the corner of her eye, she saw an unmistakable object in the viewport, but Torin was faster, forcing the ship down. The violent maneuver forced her head back and forth sharply, banging her into unconsciousness.

"Damn!" He dove down further to avoid the asteroids.

"Where the hell did that come from?" He glanced sideways and noticed Gadara's head hung limply forward. Thank God she had her harness on. He had to concentrate. The smaller pieces of the asteroid were everywhere and could damage the ship. He dodged them using all the maneuvers he could think of. Finally, he realized this whole exercise was just flight time. He punched in the coordinates to return to the original location. He flipped the transporter around abruptly and headed back to find the Concordance.

It seemed like an eternity when he returned to the spot, but there was no Concordance and no other transporters. He tried to locate the Concordance with all the sensors on. Nothing. No pings, nothing on their version of radar. Then he tried the Comm-link.

"Anyone out there? This is Training Transporter, come in."

No response. He tried several times with no luck. He reached over and brushed his hand over Gadara's hair.

She stirred. He caressed her face. "Gadara. Are you all right?"

"No. My head hurts. What happened?" She sleepily glanced at him.

"Asteroids. Was that part of the lesson plan?"

"No. Return to our initial location."

"We are here. No one is responding."

She glanced at the Nav-U-Comm. "How long have we been gone?"

"A few hours, I think." He glanced at his watch, then the clock on the Nav-U-Comm. "Oh shit!"

She sat up. "What is it?"

"My watch was set to the same time as the Nav-U-Comm when we started." He glanced at the watch, then the clock, then Gadara. "My watch is an hour ahead now."

She pulled his wrist toward her. "Oh shit! We missed the jump."

"I hope you know the way?"

"Of course I do." She reached over and typed some coordinates onto her keypad, then stopped. "You're the pilot now. How would you get us back?"

He rubbed his chin. "Hmmm." He remembered the manual and typed onto the keypad, 'location to Vestra Major.' At least, that's what he had heard her say once before, since Vaedra was their sun. "Hang on, baby, we're going for a ride."

He pushed the throttle forward and they were off.

Keely and Tremol were strapped in on the main deck of the Concordance, going through hyperspace. This was a new experience for her, so she held onto Tremol's hand, but her body felt as if it was melting into the seat back. She tried to turn toward him, but the effort was difficult. "I hope the captain and Conolly can find us," she said.

"The captain is an experienced pilot. I'm sure she can find her way home." Tremol squeezed her hand.

"Has this ever happened before?" She asked.

"What do you mean?"

"Has a part of a mission disappeared before?"

"Yes, that's how we met, remember?"

"Of course. How can I forget that? You changed my life. I mean, something like this?"

"Well, no. At least she taught her students well. They all returned safely and completed their FTMs."

"FTMs?"

"Flight time maneuvers."

The two of them had been flying for some time. Gadara looked over at Conolly. Now was the time for questions. "So, why were you on our ship?"

"You don't beat around the bush, do you?"

"I think you owe me the truth."

"I told you why."

"If you came to learn to fly our ships and teach others, then why did your general ask me to go back with him to do the same thing?"

"What?"

"You heard me, Torin Conolly. You owe me the truth."

He lowered his head. "You're absolutely right, Gadara. I came here to steal one of your smaller ships and fly it back to Earth so they could reverse engineer it."

"Why? We offered to teach you how to fly them and I am teaching you all I know about these ships. Our Military will sell you ships and help you transport them back to Earth."

"Yes, but they didn't know that when they sent me."

"Your president knew this."

"I was not sent here by the president of our country."

"Who sent you?"

"The NSA."

"And that is?"

"The National Security Agency. But it's under a clandestine operation the president isn't aware of. Besides that, they were not aware that the ships couldn't make it back to Earth."

"Are you stealing this ship?"

"No! That all came from the implants," Torin said.

"Are your people working with the greys?"

"Yes, they get a lot of tech from them."

"The greys will give you the tech they will use on you to destroy you."

"What are you talking about?"

"That's how they have operated for centuries. We've studied them and their tactics. They will use their high frequency auroral towers to control minds and take over your planet. All people with implants will be used subliminally to implement their scheme. The rest will rise in violence."

"How did you know about the towers?"

"I told you, we study our enemies' tactics. We've kept the greys out of our system for decades."

"Those towers are used to control the weather."

"And do they control the weather?"

"Sometimes."

"Where are we going, Torin?"

"We're heading to Vestra Major."

"Don't lie to me!"

"I'm telling you the truth, Gadara."

"We've missed the jump point, Torin. Where the Vaedran hell are we?"

Earth, Washington, D.C.

Mr. and Mrs. McGuire sat in front of the TV in Keely's apartment and watched the news.

"For further news on the violence and unrest across the country, we take you to the White House," the news anchor said.

"Besides the National Guard, the President has authorized the military to take action against the domestic terrorists plaguing the country," the reporter announced.

"Has the President added any more states to the mandatory curfew list?" the anchor asked.

"Yes, besides the twenty-four already on the list, he's added Nebraska, Kansas, Ohio, and Tennessee. The President further warned that the terrorists violating the law will be shot. He's hoping this warning will curtail the violence."

"Oh my God," Mrs. McGuire said. "I can't believe all that's happened since Keely left."

"Shhh." Mr. McGuire turned the sound up.

"And now for the news around the globe," the news anchor said. "England has reported a rise in violent crimes in the last two days, coinciding with the U.S. reports. France, Germany, and Spain have also deployed their military to stop the violence raging in those countries."

Mrs. McGuire watched the scenes depicted from each locale showing the unrest, while wringing her hands.

"Keely has been gone about four days and all this happened since the exposure of the Black Government," Mr. McGuire said. He flipped the channel to another news network.

"The UFO sightings have increased across the globe, but more predominantly over Germany," another reporter said.

"I wonder what the Germans are up to?" Mrs. McGuire said.

"You think they are working with the aliens?" Mr. McGuire asked.

"According to conspiracy theories, they did during the Second World War. That's why we got all their top scientists."

"In an unprecedented move, the Justice Department has requested all those arrested for their participation in the operation and coverup of the Black Government be held without bond until further investigations are completed," a news anchor announced. "As a matter of national security, the Justice Department stated earlier, it's imperative that these individuals are kept in secure locations."

Mr. McGuire turned off the TV.

"I hope Keely and Tremol are safe wherever they are," Mrs. McGuire said.

"Yes. Now I wish we had gone with them."

"You know, I've noticed that whenever there is a UFO sighting in this country, violence erupts in that same area within a day."

"Are you sure?"

"Yes, I've been tracking the sightings for our own safety." She got up and pulled a map off the desk and opened it on the coffee table. "Look at these red dots. That's the area the UFOs were seen. The yellow dots represent where the violence has erupted."

"I wonder if the President knows this?" he asked.

"I should hope so."

❈ 18 ❈

"While you were sleeping, Gadara, I managed to avoid destroying this ship in an asteroid mine field."

"Sleeping? You think I was sleeping? You were so reckless you knocked me out!"

"I saved your ass while I was doing fucking flight time maneuvers."

"You managed to get us lost."

"We aren't lost."

All right, Torin, where are we?"

An alarm sounded.

"There you go, baby, we're entering the jump. Hang on to your pretty little ass."

She was thrown back into her seat. That ought to quiet her down. This ship handled much smoother than he anticipated. The jump seemed to take over an hour of straight pressure. His adrenaline pumped through his veins. He loved flying and this was the bomb. His first jump through hyperspace, and he was sitting next to the most beautiful woman he had ever met. He had to win back her trust somehow. Without those implants, he wasn't the same man who boarded the transporter. He no longer had a mission, but he wouldn't mind flying the wing ship when all was said and done. But would Gadara still let him? Especially now that she knew why he was here?

He reached for her hand, which was clasped tightly on the arm of the seat. She didn't fight him, but held on.

"Next stop, Timucan Space Station."

They eased out of hyperspace and she glanced over at him.

"I don't know if I should let you continue training now that I know why you are here."

"Gadara, that's no longer my mission, you've got to believe me."

"How can I trust you?"

He unbuckled his harness and leaned over the seat and kissed her. "Does that help?"

"Are you trying to seduce me?"

"Is it working?"

Gadara rolled her eyes.

"I care about you, Gadara, and I want you to know that."

"You can't continue working for people controlled by the greys. They will not stop until your planet is theirs."

"What would you like me to do, then? If I return, I'll be reprimanded for not carrying out my mission." Or worse.

"Stay with me. You would be my mate on my Mission Specialist assignment."

"Your mate?" He remembered something Eno had told him earlier.

"Yes, since we are mated."

"Wait, are you saying we are mates because we had sex?"

"In the Vaedra system, when someone takes a mate, it is for life."

"Whoa. That sounds too permanent for me." Like marriage.

"Do you mate with every woman you meet?"

"No, of course not." Since he was officially dead, he hadn't been with anyone in quite a while. Gadara was the first woman he had been alone with in years. "Look, on Earth, if we have sex with someone, it doesn't mean we are married, uh, mated."

She crossed her arms and gave him the meanest look he had ever seen. Fear crept up his spine for the first time in his life.

She clenched her jaw, unbuckled her harness and stood up.

"The trip to Vestra Major is another day from here. I'll get some sleep while you take the first watch." She turned and left him to his thoughts.

He pressed his fingers to his temples and rubbed. Mates? Why didn't she say something before they had sex? Then what? He wanted her as much as she wanted him. She could have stopped it but she didn't. And he certainly didn't want to stop either.

He wasn't the settling down type. Besides, he belonged to the U.S. Government. The NSA won't be pleased when he returns to Earth that's for sure. But who gave him those orders?

Keely and Tremol were in the eating hall when Porter approached their table. "Well, if it isn't our two liaisons," he said.

"Hello Mr. Porter. Is there anything we can do for you?" Keely asked.

"I was just wondering if you took care of that problem you had with Mr. Conolly?

"Why is that?" Tremol asked.

"Well, I haven't seen him on board this ship and you haven't confined me to my room in days."

"Everything is taken care of Mr. Porter," she said. She watched as he moved to another table.

"What was that about?" Tremol asked.

"I don't know, but now I feel he is up to something. Did you find anything when you had his room searched?"

"No. Nothing unusual."

"Do you think Conolly and Captain Gadara will catch up to us before we get to Timucan?"

"If it were me, I would head straight to Timucan Space Station. We will be there for an entire day, so if they are a little behind, they will catch up there." Tremol said.

Gadara converted the back seat of the transporter into a bed, pulling out some blankets from the storage compartments overhead. Conolly had no choice but to fly straight to Timucan but he couldn't do it without sleep.

She knew better than to give her heart to a reckless man of his looks and caliber. She punched the pillows into submission, but she wanted to punch Torin instead. Her heart ached but she would hide the pain. After all, she had gone through this before.

Earthens had strange ideas about relationships. The whole point is to get to know someone to determine if they are the one you want to spend a lifetime with. If he is not the type to do that, then she would get over him. Eventually.

After the first couple hours, his excitement waned. He loved flying, but without scenery, it got boring. All he thought about was Gadara. The look she gave him scared him. The night of passion they shared was something worth savoring. But for a lifetime? Marriage sounded so final.

The computer system they had on these ships was incredible. What would he do for the rest of the trip? And when would Gadara relieve him? After four hours? After eight? He missed her company already. She was so good looking. The thought of her soft flesh under his made his body react, just thinking about her. Damn. Now his body missed her.

He had to put thoughts of her out of his mind. The U.S. Government owned him. He had no life, especially after the government told him he was listed as dead. There was nothing he could do and nothing to look forward to except the next assignment. How could he have a relationship with a woman when he couldn't even tell her where he worked?

The next couple hours were agonizing, until Gadara walked into the Nav-U-Comm. She handed him a cup.

"What's this?"

"Capu. It will help you wake up."

"Are you here to relieve me?"

"Yes."

"Then you drink it. I need to get some sleep," he said.

"Don't mind if I do." She took a sip of the beverage.

Watching her triggered something in him. Like a familiar scene or something he'd like to see again. He unhooked his harness and stretched. He reached for her and pulled her close.

She glared at him. "I thought you didn't like relationships." She said, clutching her capu.

"I didn't say that." He leaned in for the kiss.

She pulled away. "If you want to kiss me, you'll have to take me as your mate."

"What?"

"You heard me." She stepped around him and sat in the pilot's seat.

He blinked a couple times then scratched his head. *What just happened?* He stood there, dumbfounded.

"See you in four," Gadara said. She put on her harness and took over control of the ship.

Reluctantly, he headed to the back of the ship. There he saw a compartment, he thought was a wall, opened up to reveal a small galley. Beside the galley was the bed. He lay on the bed and curled up in the blankets. They smelled of Gadara. The thought of her the night before, wrapped around him, brought a smile to his face. He wouldn't mind more of that. Who was he fooling, anyway. He was lonely as hell and she was the best thing that ever happened to him. He eventually went to sleep, but she was the last thing on his mind.

❧ 19 ☙

Gadara put Torin Conolly out of her mind. He was an amusement for a short time, no more. If Earthens treat something intimate as mating as a casual fling, she could too. But at her age, no one in Vestra Major would have her as a mate. Most people thought she wanted a career in the military above a home and happiness with a mate. She would let them cling to their fantasies.

Now that Torin was after their ships, she would not teach him to fly the wing ship. Her class was almost over and she would finish with the space station landings. The last part on Vestra Major would be FTMs. She would apply for the Special Missions Team once her grades were turned in.

She had the perfect place for Torin Conolly, in the meantime, but he wouldn't like it one bit.

～

The alarm on Torin's watch went off. He had to relieve Gadara. He found something in the galley that resembled space food and brought it to her, along with some water.

"What, no capu?"

"About that. I don't know how to make it." He handed her a bottle of water and a couple tubes of space food.

"You'll never make it in the Vaedran Military. They teach us how to prepare edible meals with this stuff."

"You'll have to show me."

Gadara unfastened her harness and stood up. She took her food and water and leaned close to his face. "In your dreams, I'll show you," she whispered. Her sexy voice sent chills up his spine.

He sat down and watched her walk off. Seeing her figure through the sheerness of the fabric brought back memories of their one night of passion. His body reacted to the thought.

This was going to be a long four hours. He sucked down the tubes of food paste and chugged his water. Before he finished his meal, Gadara returned with two cups. She handed him one.

"Thank you," he said. He gave her a wink and she smiled. He tasted the coffee-flavored brew. "I needed this."

"Yes, I know. You'll be landing at Timucan in four hours. It can be tricky landing this size ship in their hubs. I'll be back in time to guide you through it."

Before she left, he grabbed her hand. "Gadara, I'm sorry if I hurt you."

She hesitated before pulling away, but said nothing.

He had hurt her more than he realized. When he first tried to please her, she was surprised. He loved her reactions to his kindness. Would he ever see that response again?

He finished off his tubes of food paste and water, then enjoyed the capu. It was pretty good considering it wasn't really coffee, but it did have the caffeine he needed.

Just as she said, Gadara returned in about three hours and

sat beside him. His heart beat a little faster when he saw her enter the room.

"Do you need more capu?" she asked.

"I'd love some, thank you."

She got up and headed back to the galley, taking all the trash he had accumulated with her.

When she returned, he realized he had looked forward to seeing her again.

"Here you go," she said. She handed him the cup of capu. He sipped it slowly. She put on her harness and drank her capu in silence.

"Tell me about Timucan Space Station, Gadara."

"Timucan is located between Vestra Major and Persus. It's run by the I.S.P."

"What's that?"

"The I.S.P. is the Interplanetary Space Patrol, a quasi-military group that protects the planets within the Vaedra system, and the military protects beyond the planets."

"Got it. Now how should I approach the station?"

"There are several tiers where you can land. The Concordance is too big to land, so they will send transporters to the station where everyone can take leave for a day or for several hours."

Through the viewport, the station came into sight. "Wow, that looks big from here," he said.

"It is huge. It's practically a city in the sky."

"Have you been there before?"

"Of course, many times."

"What's your favorite thing about the station?" he asked, trying to get her to open up.

"I like the gaming room. There are several games going on at once that you can participate in or watch. There's food and drink there as well."

"What kind of games?"

"My favorite is stickit, then there's slam, and a game called knockout."

He watched as she explained the games and the layout of the place. Her face lit up when she talked. She was actually very entertaining and he found he really enjoyed her company.

As they approached the Space Station, he got a glimpse of the landing hubs.

"You'll have to slow down to approach," she said.

He complied and got the ship to a hover and set it down on the hub, parallel to the station. A tube extended up to the side of the ship and covered the doorway with an airtight suction.

"Once the airlock is secure, we can leave the ship. Be sure to take your helmet."

He reached up and pulled out two helmets and handed one to her.

"Is the Concordance here?"

"Yes, but it's hovering out above the Space Station. Some of her transporters are here."

"So what happens now?"

"I'll contact the Concordance and let them know we are here," she said. She hit the comm-link. "Captain Gadara to Concordance, come in." No response. "Concordance, come in. This is Captain Gadara of training transporter, come in." No response.

He glanced at her. "You know, we were hit by some of those smaller asteroids. Maybe the comm-link was damaged."

Her eyes widened. "Well, in that case, we head inside, take leave for a few hours and search for others from the ship."

"Sounds like a plan to me."

Gadara put on her helmet, so he did the same, securing it to his shoulders. He watched her open the ship's door and followed her out. They walked through the secured tube and into the airlock before removing their helmets.

"We can leave the helmets here," she said. She handed the helmets to a clerk who handed her two numbers.

"Don't lose your number. That's how you get your helmet back." She started to walk off then stopped.

"What's the matter?" he asked.

"From now on, you call me Captain Gadara." She touched his chest. He felt a tug in his heart at her words.

"Yes, Captain Gadara." It sounded strange now that they had been intimate. He missed her intimacy already.

He followed her to the gaming room and they got some food and ale, while watching others play stickit. It was a lot like pool, but the table was round.

After they had finished eating, she glanced around the room. Then she turned to him. "How about a game of stickit?"

"You and me?"

She nodded.

"I'd love to."

She paid for the food and drink and paid for a table. In a few minutes, they played stickit.

While he took a shot, he heard a male voice behind him.

"Where the hell have you been?"

"Eno!" He turned to see his roommate, but Eno was not smiling.

"Everyone was concerned about you and the captain. Where is she?"

"She's right…" He turned back to the table, but she was gone. "We were playing stickit, I swear. I don't know where she's at now." *Where the hell was she?*

"You better find her or you'll be spending time in the brig."

Why was he so mad? "She's here somewhere. I'll find her."

He set his stick down and searched the crowded room.

~

"Genesis!" Gadara called out.

Genesis turned at the sound of her name and found her waving.

"Hello, Captain. How may I be of service to you?" Genesis asked. Beside her was her mate, Adam. Gadara had met both of them when they initially traveled from Vestra Major to Earth. She noticed Adam had what Torin referred to as a beard, but it was fuller since she had first met him. She studied his face.

"Does that hair on your face hurt?" she asked.

"No. Not at all," Adam said.

"May I touch it?"

He glanced at Genesis. She nodded.

"It is soft. Do you like this facial hair?" she asked.

"I grew the beard so I wouldn't look like my father, Dram. He was a wanted man and there may be people out there who don't know he's been captured and spending the rest of his life on Plumaris," Adam said.

"I like it because it tickles my neck," Genesis added.

"Yes, I can see how that would be pleasurable for you when mating."

Adam changed colors from white to pink instantly, around his neck and face.

"Do all Earthens change colors like you?" she asked.

"He calls it blushing. He does that whenever he's embarrassed," Genesis said.

"Okay, let's not make a big deal about it," he said.

"So, what can I help you with, Captain Gadara?" Genesis asked.

"I've had a head injury and was hoping you could heal me."

"I would love to." Genesis glanced around and found a quiet booth. "Shall we?" She gestured to the seats.

She headed for the booth. Adam sat opposite the two of them. "It's right here." She touched the tender spot on the back of her head.

"Oh, yes. I feel it. How did it happen?"

"Conolly flew us through an asteroid field, dodging the

rocks, but when he did, I banged my head on the seat and passed out."

"Goodness." Genesis held the back of her head tenderly and began her prayer chant in her native tongue.

She sat still, her eyes closed, trying to relax. It was only moments until the pain subsided, then was gone. She waited until Genesis stopped her prayer chanting.

"How do you feel now?"

She turned around and hugged Genesis. "I feel wonderful. Thank you."

"You're welcome."

"How long have you been here?" she asked.

"We've been here a couple hours," Adam said.

"Yes, we're waiting on Keely and Lieutenant Tremol. We will be heading to Vestra Major with them."

"Why is that?"

"They are going ahead of the Concordance to line up the meetings with the Earthen counterparts," Genesis said.

"The admiral suggested that the delegates stay aboard the ship at night and fly into Vestra Major in the day to save time and money," Adam said.

"Money?" She had not heard that word before.

"You call it Kashis, I think," he said.

"Oh, yes. That makes sense."

Keely and Tremol walked up to their booth.

"Hello, Captain," Keely said. "We're so glad you're safe."

"Why wouldn't I be?"

"Well, we were all worried about you."

"Why?"

"Because you didn't make it back before the jump," Tremol said.

"Did the rest of my class make it?"

"Yes. Everyone but you."

"Then I taught them well. The asteroid field was unexpected, throwing Conolly off course, but he managed to find his way here."

"That's good news," Tremol added.

"Unfortunately, the bad news is, Conolly was trying to steal one of our ships. That's why he was sent."

"All that's changed, hasn't it? Since the implants were removed?" Keely asked.

"I'm not sure. I don't know if I can trust him. And I certainly will not continue teaching him how to fly the very ship he was sent to steal." He didn't have to tell her the truth. He could have lied about why he was really here, so isn't that a point in his favor?

"What happens now?" Genesis asked.

"I think the best thing to do is turn this over to the admiral, for his decision," she said.

"Will you be returning him to the Concordance yourself, then?" Tremol asked.

"Yes. We may have suffered damage from the asteroids. Our comm-link didn't work. Could you please let the admiral know that we made it back safely?"

"I'd be happy to, Captain." Tremol glanced at his chrono. "It's time for us to leave," he said. Everyone slid off the bench seats into the aisle.

She hugged Genesis again and thanked her for her healing. She reached out her hand to shake Adam's outstretched hand. But when he touched her hand, he squeezed tighter than was comfortable and didn't let go. He stared at her but wasn't really looking at her. She waved her free hand in front of his face and he didn't flinch or look away.

"What's happening?" Keely asked.

"Are you having a premonition?" Tremol asked.

He kept squeezing and shaking her hand, staring into space.

"Adam!" Genesis said sharply.

He blinked then looked around. "Oh my God!" he said.

"What happened?" she asked, after he had finally released her hand. She flexed her fingers to get the circulation going.

"I saw the Earth surrounded by space ships, alien space ships, and they are shooting down at the planet."

"What are you talking about?" she asked.

"Adam has premonitions, which have all come true," Tremol explained.

"We've got to save the Earth," Adam said.

"Captain, can you relay that information to the admiral? We've got to head down to Vestra Major now and set up the meetings. I'll brief everyone there," Tremol said.

"Yes, of course."

"Thank you, Captain," Keely said. They all left.

She headed back to the stickit table, but Conolly was gone. She searched for him all over the gaming room but there was no sign of him. That's odd. She headed back to her ship.

When she handed the clerk her number to retrieve her helmet, she touched the woman's shoulder. "Did you see the pilot I came in with? Tall, good looking, Caucus?"

She glanced at her numbered ticket. "Yes. He claimed his helmet and left with a Chromian pilot and two guards."

"Thank you." What in the worlds? She decided to head back to the Concordance and see what had happened. The Chromian most likely was Eno, but the two guards? What was that about?

She fired up the engines and when everything was ready, contacted the hub control. "Training Transporter to hub, permission to exit the hub?" No response. She slammed her fist hard against the comm-link and tried again. "Training Transporter requests permission to exit the hub."

"Control to Training Transporter, permission granted. Your comm-link is breaking up. Advise repairs."

She headed straight to the Concordance and went through the same problems she had at the hub.

"Concordance, this is Training Transporter, requesting permission to land." No response.

She slammed her fist against the comm-link twice.

"…identify yourself."

"Concordance, this is Training Transporter. Having problems with comm-link. Need permission to land."

"Glad to hear your voice, Captain Gadara. Permission granted."

She berthed her ship and exited her transporter. By the time she got up to the tech area, ten minutes had gone by.

"Have my ship evaluated for asteroid damage, especially the comm-link system," she said to the Systems Tech.

"I'll get right on it, Captain. Glad you're back safe."

She decided to see the admiral and let him know what she learned from Adam. Then she would fill him in on what she learned about Conolly.

She touched her communicator on her chrono. "Captain Gadara to Admiral Esrith, come in."

"Captain, are you all right?"

"Yes, Admiral. I'm perfectly fine. I have some information for you. Where are you?"

"I'm in the brig area. Can you meet me here?"

"Of course, Admiral. On my way."

Torin turned his back to Eno and Eno cut his restraints.

"You'll remain here until the admiral lets you go." Eno said. He closed the cage. "Don't let him out for anyone except the admiral," Eno ordered the two guards who had accompanied them.

Conolly knew he was in big trouble. It was all a misunderstanding. Gadara was somewhere in the gaming room, but Eno wouldn't allow him to look for her anymore. Where did she go, anyway? The cleansing compartment? He hadn't thought to look there. Eno was angry with him. Did Eno have feelings for Gadara? She was at least ten years older than Eno. She was more his type than Eno's, anyway.

He heard someone approach and it was verified by the guards snapping to attention. Coming down the hall were the Joint Chiefs of Staff of the Army and the Air Force, along with the admiral. He saluted them and they returned the salute.

"It can't be," General Stevens of the Air Force said. "I was at your funeral. You died in a crash of an experimental aircraft."

"I told you, Ben." The general turned to him.

"Explain your presence here," General Stevens said.

"Sir, I—"

"That's classified," Claud Porter said. He came down the hall behind the three men. "Don't say a word, Conolly."

"Or what? You'll kill me?" He didn't know who this guy was, but he was tired of sneaking around and lying. He'd already hurt Gadara and Eno. He'd lost their trust and for what? The NSA couldn't have what they wanted anyway. And he didn't even know who gave him those orders or why.

The two military men turned toward Porter. "Who the hell are you?" General Thompson demanded.

"I'm with NSA. I'm Claud Porter."

"I thought you didn't know Mr. Conolly," the Admiral said.

"Who told you that?"

"Our two liaisons."

"Well, I didn't give them all the facts since it's classified."

"So you lied to them?" The admiral pressed him.

"No. I told them I knew of Torin Conolly, that's all."

"Start talking, Porter, or you will be in a cell of your own," the admiral said.

"Is that how you treat a delegate from Earth?"

"When it seems you are withholding pertinent information and being difficult, I can do whatever I deem necessary for the safety of my crew. Right now, you pose a serious problem." The admiral nodded and the two guards came up behind Porter and escorted him into the cell next to Conolly's. When they searched him, they found a small, hand-held device and handed it to the admiral.

"Well, what's this?" the admiral asked.

"That's personal property," Porter said. "You have no right to take that from me."

"Really? Well, it looks like a weapon to me," the admiral said. He placed it in his pocket. Porter clenched his jaw and said nothing more.

"Well, Conolly?" General Stevens of the Air Force said.

"I don't know this gentleman, Mr. Porter." He gestured to the cell next to his. "I do work for the NSA and NASA, flying experimental aircraft." He thought he saw some movement behind the three men, but couldn't be sure what it was.

"My best friend was killed in a crash that I witnessed. The NSA and agents of the Black Government approached me and asked if I'd like to fly some other experimental aircraft. I said sure, but there was a catch. They would write me off as dead and I could never see my family and friends again."

"Who was that they buried?" General Stevens asked.

"I really don't know, sir. Unless it was an empty casket."

"Then what happened?" the Army general asked.

"I flew space ships, rockets, jets, and anything else they could get their hands on. One ship, you had to fly with your mind. I wouldn't recommend it, though."

"Why not?" General Stevens asked.

"If you get distracted for any reason, you could easily crash it. I prefer something with hands-on technology."

"Who built this craft?"

"The greys are working hand in hand with the Black Government. They give us technology and we let them experiment on our people."

"The hell you say!" General Thompson said.

"The abductions of humans has been going on for years, sir. It's not a made-up story by crazies. It's real. They use implants to control them as well as other things like impregnating women to carry a child mixing our DNA and theirs. Then they abduct them again and remove the child to incubate it in their labs."

"You've gone too far, Conolly. You will regret this," Claud Porter said.

"I regret that I even know this stuff, Mr. Porter. I regret that I ever made that deal with your people." He turned toward General Stevens. "This Porter guy is not with the NSA but with a clandestine group so secret that even the President doesn't know about it."

"He's outed the Black Government, Conolly. All those who participated in it will be arrested if they haven't already by the time we return." General Stevens turned toward Admiral Esrith.

"I would suggest that you keep Mr. Porter locked up until we return to Earth, Admiral. For your safety."

"I agree," the admiral said.

Conolly caught another glimpse of someone moving behind the three men, but couldn't tell who it was. The three men left and he was alone with his thoughts, and Mr. Porter next door.

"You sealed your fate, Conolly," Porter said.

"Yes, I know. I did that the day I agreed to work with the NSA."

"There's something you don't know about that accident, boy."

"Oh? Suppose you fill me in."

"The day of the crash, you both died."

"Yes, that's the story they used to keep family from doing any digging."

"No. You both were killed in that crash, but you were the only one they could revive."

❧ 21 ❧

"What the hell are you talking about?" Torin demanded.

"They altered your memories. The greys gave you life, but changed your memories so you would remember seeing your friend die in that crash, when it was really the two of you who died."

"What?"

"They didn't talk you into working in that program. You were already in it, you just didn't know it. They changed your memories so you would think it all came about from the crash. You had been in the clandestine training group from the start. You were to steal that wing ship and return it so they could reverse engineer it."

"Do you know how stupid that sounds?" He remembered Gadara's words.

"What are *you* talking about?" Porter asked.

"They offered to sell us those ships and teach us to fly them. We don't have to steal anything. Besides, only the transporters can make the trip back to Earth, so you're wasting your time."

He crossed his arms and leaned against the back of his cell. How could Porter say they had both died? That was the lie they wanted everyone to believe. Could it be true?

How was he going to make it up to Gadara and Eno? They had become his only friends. Now, he was alone once again. Something he was used to, but never enjoyed. He walked to the front of the cage and held on to the bars. He leaned his forehead against the cold metal. How long would he be stuck in here? What was the admiral planning to do to him? And what would they do to him when he returned to Earth empty-handed?

When the admiral rounded the corner near the stairs, he saw her. "Captain Gadara! Are you all right?"

"Yes, of course. Why is everyone asking me that?"

"We thought Conolly abducted you."

"Why would you think that?"

"You weren't at the meet point."

"We came across an asteroid field in our FTMs and Conolly managed to keep us intact and got us back to the meet point, but we hit a small worm hole and were thrown off by an hour."

"I'm so glad you're safe. You remember General Thompson?"

"Yes sir." she offered her hand.

"And this is General Stevens of the Air Force," Esrith said.

She offered her hand to him as well. "Glad to meet you, sir."

"This is the one I told you about, Ben. She could train your pilots to fly these ships."

"Let's all go to my office," Esrith said. He ushered them to the people mover. They stopped on level one and got out.

"This way," Esrith gestured.

His office was not big enough for the four of them, so she stood, while the two generals sat opposite Esrith at his desk. Esrith set something on his desk, near the container with the implants. As soon as he did, the implants started vibrating.

"What the hell is that?" Thompson stood to get a better look.

"Did you take that from Porter?" she asked.

"Yes."

"Porter's the one who has been controlling Conolly," she said.

"It appears that way," Esrith said.

"What is that?" Stevens asked. He pointed to the container of implants.

"That's what my Chief Medical Officer, Conn, removed from Conolly not too long ago. The greys use telepathy to control people. Apparently, they've devised this apparatus so that humans can control other humans."

"This is disturbing after hearing what Conolly told us," Thompson said.

"Whatever you do, do not release Porter except to the President. He would be key to his investigation," Stevens said.

"That is not a problem, gentlemen."

"Admiral, if I may?" she said.

"Go ahead, Captain."

"I speak on behalf of Lieutenant Tremol." She glanced at the admiral and then the two generals. "Adam Davis, one of our guests, has premonitions that come true."

"Is that the young man who brought all of you to Earth?" Stevens asked.

"Yes, he is," Admiral Esrith said.

"Adam had a premonition when I spoke to him. He saw space ships surrounding the Earth and firing upon it with their weapons."

"Good God! We have no defense for that," General Thompson said.

"From what Genesis and Adam shared with me during their briefing, the greys have been working with your shadow government. This shadow government thought they could threaten us, but I assure you gentlemen, this is a star destroyer. We can, and have, turned desolate planets into asteroids. We have fought the greys and kept them away from our system."

"Will you help us?" General Thompson asked.

"Of course, but I must bring this matter up before the Council of Nations. We will be over Vestra Major tomorrow, and can call the Council for an emergency meeting. You'll also be able to meet key people who can work with you while we are here."

"Great! I look forward to this meeting," General Stevens said.

"Me, too. Thank you, Admiral," Thompson said. They shook hands and the two men left.

Finally, she could tell the admiral what she learned from Conolly.

"If I may ask, sir, why is Conolly in the brig?"

"Eno brought him here because he couldn't account for your whereabouts."

"But I'm right here. Nothing happened. In fact, I would pass him on his flight skills. If it weren't for his fast reactions, we could have been killed. Instead, I suffered minor injuries."

"Minor injuries? What happened?"

"He dove hard to avoid a collision and I hit my head on the back of the seat. I'm fine now. Genesis healed me. Conolly managed to get us to the meet point and then here without my help, so he did extremely well for one who hasn't flown in this area of space. However, after I tell you what I learned, you may want to keep him in the brig."

"When we get back to Earth, Conolly, you'll be court marshalled," Porter said.

"On what grounds?"

"Releasing classified information."

He uncrossed his arms and moved to the bars between their cages. "Seems to me, you are a wanted man since you work for the Black Government."

"You do too, Conolly."

"After what you told me, I think I'll turn state's evidence. I'm already considered dead, so you and your people can't hurt me anymore. I've already lost everything that was dear to me."

Even more, his friendship with Eno and Gadara. Gadara would be harder to get over. He didn't think he would miss her, but he had. Knowing that he hurt her with his flippant manner bothered him more than he realized. Any man would want to be in a relationship with a woman as beautiful and competent as her. And after flying the transporter, he realized she was more fun than flying alone.

He thought about their brief affair and how passionate she was. He wouldn't mind waking up with her in his arms again. But he had to face reality. His future was no longer in his hands. In fact, with the Black Government outed, he could spend his life in prison. He had been part of that mess for years as a lowly pilot. It was the higher ups that called the shots and they worked with the greys.

While the admiral was deciding what to do about Torin Conolly, Gadara finished her training on landings at the Space Station with the rest of her class. This was their last official class and the rest would be flight time over Vestra Major.

She put Torin out of her mind. She was a captain and she acted like it. She would have time later to dwell on her feelings if she felt so inclined.

It was late when she returned from the training. She had her reports to write about each man that she would turn in to the admiral. On her way to her room, she ran into General Stevens of the U.S. Air Force.

"Hello, General," she said.

"Captain Gadara! I was just thinking about you."

"Oh? I hope it wasn't anything bad."

"Not at all. In fact, I think the suggestion that General Thompson made about you teaching my pilots how to fly is a great idea. What do you think about that?"

"Well, sir, I'm flattered, but I had already put in for our Mission Specialist Team that would explore outer planets in nearby star systems. I'm about as high up as I want to go. After Captain, there's more paperwork and no flight time."

"I totally understand that. I only get to fly my private jet and not very often anymore."

"May I ask you a question about Conolly, sir?"

"Yes, of course."

"What happens to him when he returns to Earth?"

"Well, he would be arrested and jailed, along with all the

others who participated in the Black Government. Once the investigations are over, that will determine his fate."

"What happens if he doesn't return to Earth?"

"Now that's a good question. I don't know, because he was considered dead. It would open up a whole can of worms if he did return."

"Worms? What is that, sir?" she asked.

"It would make a big mess for everyone to sort out."

"Thank you, sir."

"What has the admiral decided, since Conolly was considered a stowaway to begin with?"

"He's deliberating on that as we speak. Technically, he gave a name that was on the list that the liaisons had."

"Keep me informed, would you? And let me know what you think about training our people. We could keep you at captain's pay or promote you, whichever you prefer. We need someone of your caliber for training purposes." He saluted her and left.

One way or the other, Torin was kunnarled, either by his own people, or by hers.

Gadara finished her reports and sent her information to the Special Missions Team, headquartered in Vestra Major. She headed to the Officers Lounge. Of course, she ran into Eno and his father.

"Hello boys!" She waved. The two men sat at a table, drinking. Admiral Esrith waved her over.

"Are you just starting or finishing?" she asked.

"We're right in the middle," Eno said. "I'm so glad you're all right."

"Thank you for your concern, Eno. I didn't know you cared about me."

"We all do, Captain. After all, you trained all the pilots on this ship. I think we'd all tear Conolly limb from limb if he had hurt you."

"Well, the concern is appreciated, but that gesture terrifies me, just thinking about it," she said. Especially since those limbs were wrapped around her recently.

The admiral had gestured to the barkeep and he brought her an ale.

"Are we drinking lighter tonight?" she asked.

"Yes, since I have a heavy decision to make," the admiral said.

"Captain," Eno began. "Aren't you the one who suggested we throw Conolly off the ship and cast him into space?"

"I guess that was me, wasn't it?"

"I say, keep him locked up," Eno said.

"What good would that do, Eno?" she asked.

"Teaches him a lesson."

"A lesson about what?" she asked.

"Not to mess with the Vaedran Military."

"I think he got that message when you hauled him to the brig, Eno," the admiral said.

"I just spoke to General Stevens," she said. "If Conolly returns to Earth, he would be locked up along with all those from the Black Government for participating with them."

"And if he stays here, he would be locked up as a stowaway in our prisons on Vestra Major," Eno said.

"Either way, the man is kunnarled," the admiral said.

That's what she had thought. Was there no way out for him? He had told her the truth and he didn't have to.

"I was just beginning to like the man," Eno said.

She glanced at him as he took a long sip of his ale. "I really don't have many friends, and he was becoming one to me. Hell, he even did my laundry," Eno continued.

"That says a lot," the admiral said.

"Yes, and he brought me food when I worked past the mid-day meal. It was totally unexpected," Gadara added. Then she thought of the times he made her smile, and the time they both did laundry. The tempting whispers to her mouth that made her want to kiss him, and the way he made her feel when they mated.

She heard a commotion behind her and turned to see four

U.S. Military men standing in the entrance to the lounge. The admiral stood up and greeted them. "Come join us, gentlemen."

Eno and she stood, grabbing extra chairs from other tables. Eno finally grabbed an extra table and she helped him move it in place. When they sat down again, she sat across from Eno and the others sat closer to the Admiral.

General Thompson introduced the Admiral of the U.S. Navy, Joint Chiefs of Staff, Admiral Halsey, and Admiral Johnson of the U.S. Space Force and newest member of the Joint Chiefs of Staff.

"Admiral Esrith, we've come to talk to you about Torin Conolly," General Thompson said.

The barkeep approached their table and took drink orders. She glanced at her ale and then the four military men.

"Make mine a Detonator," she said. She finished off her ale and handed him the empty bottle.

"Sure thing, Captain."

"I'll take one as well," Eno said.

All the others had ordered ale. That was fine with her. She needed something stronger if they were talking about Torin.

After the barkeep left, Admiral Esrith turned to Thompson. "What can I help you with, General?"

"Well, sir, maybe we can help you. You see, we've been comparing notes about Conolly and Admirals Halsey and Johnson were given different briefings. In light of what Captain Gadara said, we all need to be on the same page when it comes to the security of our nation."

"Yes, sir. After your appearance on Earth, everything has changed. We need to keep in mind that while each of us heads up a large and different organization, we need to be cohesive in our approach to national security," Admiral Johnson said.

"What do you know about the Draconians?" Admiral Halsey asked.

Admiral Esrith's eyes widened. Gadara's heart rate shot up and Eno swung his full attention to Halsey.

"They are an evil race of lizard-like creatures who can change their looks to appear to be more human. Like the greys, they want to control other planets, using up the life forms on that planet until they no longer serve their purposes. Don't tell me you have Draconians on Earth?"

"I'm afraid they have infiltrated the military industrial complex, Admiral. They are controlling the shadow government," Halsey said.

"Yes, but there are the Nordics which have contacted some of our people and helped them develop weapons and space vehicles that have moved us into the future," Johnson said.

"The Nordics?" Admiral Esrith asked.

"That's what we've been calling them. I think they come from the Pleiades."

"Oh, the Pleiadians. Yes, we have treaties and agreements with them. They are the ones who taught us. Thank God for that."

"General Stevens and I just learned that we have a fleet of ships that have been working with the 'Nordics' in fighting the Draconians in space. They are due for ship upgrades since they've been gone since the 1980s," General Thompson said.

The barkeep brought the drinks. She gulped down a lot of her drink, thinking of the possibility of fighting the Draconians. "Bring me another," she said. She noticed the others looking at her.

The admiral glanced her way and then back to General Thompson. "How can you help us with Torin Conolly?" he asked.

"We believe Conolly was used by the greys and possibly the Draconians to learn about other space craft and reverse engineer those crafts for their own purposes," Thompson said.

"Yes, and we have some specific questions to ask him about his involvement that will let us know whether or not he was used in a program that wiped the memories of military personnel and used age regression to restore them back to their late twenties," Admiral Johnson said.

Age regression? Where had she heard that before? Was it from the Pleiadians? They never appearred to age, but they wouldn't wipe people's memories.

"We would like to question him after he gives us a statement of everything he remembers from the time of his enlistment," Admiral Halsey said.

"Yes, Admiral, I was at Torin Conolly's funeral, but it was over twenty years ago. That would make him closer to fifty years old. As you can see, he appears to be in his early thirties," General Stevens said.

Fifty? How could that be? Would Conn be able to tell his true age? She finished off her first Detonator as the barkeep brought her second drink.

Eno touched her forearm. "Are you all right?" he asked.

"Fine. I'm fine," she lied. She had mated with a man twenty years her senior. But all his moves and mannerisms were very much those of a younger man.

"Can you arrange for us to meet with him and record his statements?" Admiral Johnson asked.

"Of course. After we have our morning briefing, we can use the map room. I'll have everything set up for you. Let's say 1100 hours?"

"That works for us, Admiral," General Thompson said.

"I have a question," she blurted out. All their faces turned toward her. "After all your questions, what will you do to Torin Conolly?"

"In light of what's happening on Earth and if he was used by our government in unethical ways, I believe it would be better if he remained here in the Vaedra system. All records of him on Earth show that he is dead. Bringing him back to Earth would unleash a lot of ethics questions that would take years to sort out and he would probably remain in prison while they figure that out," Admiral Johnson said.

"Thank you for your time, Admiral Esrith." General Thompson stood first. Then the others joined him. Esrith stood and they all shook hands before leaving the three of them alone.

"What will you do with Conolly when they finish with him?" Eno asked the question she had wanted to voice herself.

"I was hoping one of you would convince him to join the Vaedran Military." He looked at Eno and her.

"I have suggested the Special Missions Team to him," she said.

"Well, unless he joins us, he will be serving time in the prison on Vestra Major.

❧ 2 3 ❧

Gadara headed to the brig. She knew what she had to do. Now there were two people in the brig. Conolly had his own cell, but no privacy. She stopped the guard in the hall.

"I need to borrow your stun weapon," she said.

"Captain?" He saluted her.

"That's not a request, that's an order."

"Yes, Captain." He unholstered his weapon and handed it to her.

"I'll take the yav as well." She held her hand out to him. He handed her the yav to the cells.

"Now, turn your back until I tell you otherwise."

The guard did what he was told.

She walked up to the cell and shot Porter and he slumped over.

"What did you do that for?" Conolly asked.

"Shhh." She unlocked the door and pulled him to her into a kiss. He reciprocated, no questions asked, wrapping his arms around her. She liked that about him.

She walked up behind the guard and shoved his weapon

into his holster. "Close your eyes and count to ten." She stuffed the yav into his hand while he counted. She was gone before he counted to five.

They were in her quarters and she pulled Conolly into a kiss. He didn't ask any questions, but kissed her back with more passion than she remembered the first time. Slowly, her unicrin came apart while she tried to remove his.

She pulled away slightly. "This isn't going to work."

"It's working so far."

She pointed to the floor. "We're both wearing boots."

Conolly bent down and untied her boots before removing his own shoes. Then he surprised her by kissing her thighs and moving up to her abdomen. The pleasure and anticipation he gave her from his tender kisses made her determined to keep him for herself. He continued up her body, slowly, until he was at her lips.

"You are my mate, Torin Conolly, whether you like it or not. I claim you for myself."

"I give you total control over me, Gadara, as your mate. Now and forever."

She wrapped her arms around him and smothered him with kisses.

Hours later, they lay together in her bed. His arms wrapped around her middle.

"What will happen to me, Gadara?"

"Your military men will come for you in the morning. They will ask you for your statement and then question you."

"Will they take me back to Earth?"

"No. You belong to me now. When I go to the Special Missions Team, you will be a part of that, with me."

"How long do we have together?"

"We have a lifetime, Torin, but we have a few more hours until I must return you to the brig."

She turned to face him. He pulled her into another passionate kiss and they continued making love until they both passed out from exhaustion.

A couple hours later, they showered and dressed.

"I must get you back to the brig before the admiral comes for you."

When they reached the hall to the brig, a different guard stood there.

"Where's the guard who was here last night?" she said to the new guard.

"He was found derelict in his duties and was removed. Hey, aren't you the prisoner that escaped?" he said to Torin.

"No prisoner escaped. I let him out. I need your yav so I can return him to his cell," she said.

The guard pressed his comm. "I found the escaped —"

She yanked his comm away from him. "Did you hear what I said?"

Another guard came racing around the corner, his stun weapon out. "Hold it right there, Captain."

She raised her hands. Torin did the same. "Looks like we're in deep shit now, baby." Torin said.

In the next few moments, Gadara and Torin were locked in the cell beside Claud Porter.

~

The admiral approached the brig. Gadara and Torin stood. He was alone. This couldn't be good, Conolly thought.

First the admiral looked at Gadara and then at him. "What have you to say for yourself, Captain?"

She put her arm around him. "I've convinced Conolly to join the Special Missions Team as my mate."

Esrith raised his eyebrows then glanced at him. "Is this true, Conolly?"

"Yes, sir. I did so willingly and without regrets." He put his arm around her shoulders.

"Well, this is unexpected. What about the guard you compromised, Captain?"

"I owe him an apology, sir."

"That and you need to speak to his supervisor to clear his record."

"Yes, sir."

"Are you planning on making this mating official, Captain Gadara?"

"Yes, sir. Providing you have time this afternoon?"

The admiral looked at his chrono. "I guess I can make time for you, Captain."

"Conolly?" the admiral said.

"Yes, sir." He saluted him. The admiral saluted back.

"You're coming with me." Esrith turned to the guards. "Release them to me."

The guard saluted. "Yes, sir." He unlocked the cage and they both stepped out.

"What about me?" Porter asked.

The admiral didn't give him an answer and left. Conolly kept the pace and his tongue. He was already in trouble on Earth. He didn't want to stir up shit around here. Gadara waved as she went looking for the guard's supervisor.

The admiral pushed the button on the people mover and

they both stepped inside. They rode in silence. He wanted to ask what the hell was happening, but he thought better of it. It must be the inquisition Gadara had told him about.

They got out on the top deck. He hadn't been up here before, only heard about it from Eno. The admiral opened a door to a large meeting room. After the admiral stepped inside, he gestured for him to come in as well. There was General Thompson of the U.S. Army, and General Stevens of the Air Force. There were two other persons he hadn't met before and all of them wore U.S. Military uniforms.

"I believe you know Generals Thompson and Stevens?" the admiral said.

"Yes, sir." He turned and saluted both men.

"And this is Admiral Halsey of the U.S. Navy, and Admiral Johnson of the U.S. Space Force." Esrith said.

He turned and saluted both admirals. *He was in deep shit.*

General Stevens stepped forward. "We've had some discussion about your situation, Conolly. We can't undo what's happened to you. But your involvement with the Black Government will be valuable information to the President as he is conducting his investigation."

"Yes, sir. I want to cooperate as much as possible with what I know. After you left yesterday, Porter told me a little more about my past that was unknown to me. In fact, I deeply regret my involvement. I didn't know I was working for a different part of the U.S. Government. Everything I did, I thought I was doing for the Air Force until a year ago. That's when I found out I was working for the NSA's clandestine program, only I didn't know it before then." His heart started racing at the thought that this was the end of the line for him.

"We want you to record everything you remember about the program, the ops, the flights, anything you did from the beginning up to your arrival on this ship. Afterward, you will sign the Comm-Pad. We will all be your witnesses, and will ask you questions as we go along."

"Yes, sir." He sat at one end of a long, oval desk where recording equipment was set up. "I guess I'll start with my enlistment."

Gadara had apologized to the supervisor and the guard and made things right. She offered to buy the guard a couple drinks for the inconvenience and have them brought to his room. After she worked it out with the Officers Lounge barkeep, she felt she was done. Her reports on her student pilots were finished and turned in to Esrith's office. All that was left was flight time maneuvers on Vestra Major and that would be done tomorrow, while all the dignitaries were at meetings on Vestra Major.

She could teach Torin how to fly wing ships without worry now that he was her mate. But he needed to study tonight if he was to fly the wing ship tomorrow.

She headed to her classroom to get the Comm-Pad with the wing ship manual. It had been hours since Esrith had let them both out of the brig. She decided to see if Conolly was sent back there. By the time she got to the brig, Conolly wasn't there. The cell next to his was still occupied by one of the delegates.

"Where's Conolly?" she asked the man.

"After the Admiral came and let you both out, he hasn't returned." He glanced at his chrono. "It's been several hours now."

"Several hours?"

"Yes. I'd say he's in big trouble. He will be when he returns to Earth."

"And who are you?"

"Claud Porter with the NSA."

"Oh, so you're the one who works with the greys."

"We all do. They have the tech we need and we have something they want."

"Yes, total domination of your Earth." She turned and walked away. How could Conolly work for these people unless he didn't know what they were up to. And what was Esrith up to with Conolly for so long? How many questions could they possibly ask him?

She decided to talk to Eno. He might know what the admiral was up to. When she knocked on his door, he opened it and glanced at the Comm-Pad in her hand.

"What are you up to?" Eno asked her.

"I was going to ask you the same thing about the admiral."

"Come in." He stepped aside to let her pass.

"It's quiet without Conolly around," he said.

"Yes, I can imagine." She glanced around his small quarters. "I can see why you have the bottom bunk." There wasn't enough room on the top for someone his size.

"Have a seat." He pulled out his desk chair for her.

"I asked Conolly to join the Special Missions Team as my mate and he said yes."

24

Eno stood up and hugged her. "Congratulations!"

"Thank you."

"Have you had your ceremony yet?"

"Oh my gosh! I asked the admiral to perform the ceremony this afternoon but I haven't done anything to prepare for it."

"Don't you think it's a little late now?" Eno glanced at his chrono. "We'll be over Vestra Major any moment now."

She reached out and patted his arm. "You will be one of my witnesses, won't you?"

"Of course."

She headed out the door. All she needed was another witness and a location. She wasn't into all that ceremonial distress. But she didn't have many friends. Like Eno, she kept to herself. Torin was the only other person she had confided in besides the two Esrith men.

She headed back to her quarters to freshen up. When she opened the door, there was Torin, sitting in her easy chair, reading a Comm-Pad.

"What are you reading?" She cocked her head.

"Hello beautiful." He put the Comm-Pad down and stood to embrace her. "I missed you."

"I missed you, too."

He whispered in her ear, "I'm reading a boring manual about flying wing ships."

She pulled away and showed him the device in her hand.

"How about that. We think alike."

"I've got to plan our ceremony."

"Yeah, about that." He ran a hand through his hair. "The inquisition took so long, the admiral said he would have to postpone it until tomorrow."

"What?"

"He said he had to get these people into some very important meetings today. Something about the Earth being attacked."

"Oh no. I forgot about that. Didn't he tell you?"

"No. What's happening?"

"Adam had a premonition about the Earth being attacked by aliens."

"Okay? Who is Adam and why should I care?"

"Adam was the Earthen who worked it out so we could all go to your Earth and exchange technology. He has premonitions that have all come true." She poked his chest. "And you should care because those greys and possibly the Draconians are behind this attack. They won't stop until the Earth is theirs."

He shook his head. "I just found out today that I lost twenty years of my life. Wiped clean, like a slate. I died over twenty years ago. They were so precise. From the moment I enlisted and back, I can remember everything. But after enlistment, it was all taken from me and rewritten."

She hugged him tightly. "I love you for who you are now."

He hugged her back and hung on.

"They told me they had age-regressed me." He pulled away slightly. "You're about to be stuck in a relationship with an older man."

"As long as your parts are working as well as they are now, I'm okay with that."

An alarm sounded. Then the Admiral's voice came over the loudspeaker.

"Welcome to Vestra Major. Earth Delegates, our pilots will be taking you down to the planet to meet with your counterparts in one hour. We will begin returning you to the Concordance by 2000 hours this evening. A meal has been prepared in your honor planet-side. Enjoy your visit. We will remain here for at least another day."

"We have a choice now. We can have our ceremony here in space or on Vestra Major," she said.

"Since we met in space, I say let's do it here on the Concordance."

"You got it." Now all she needed was another witness and maybe a little something for the special day.

"I'm starving. Let's check out that dinner," Torin said.

They headed out the door to the people mover. By the time they reached deck 7, there was a line of people waiting to leave.

"I asked Eno to be one of our witnesses," she said.

"Oh, that's a great idea. How many do we need?"

"Just one more."

"Who else did you ask?"

"I don't have any friends besides you and the two Esrith men."

"Really? What about Keely or Tremol?"

"That's a great idea. They may be planet-side, greeting all the guests. I'll look for them when we get there."

After a brief wait, they loaded up on one of the transporters. When the pilot came out to remind them to wear their harnesses, she realized it was Eno.

The trip took a little over fifteen minutes. She and Torin got off and looked for Keely and Tremol.

"There they are," Torin said. He pointed to a couple greeting people at the door of a spacious indoor garden in the heart of Sentinel City. Across from the garden was the tallest building, the Capitol. It was completely round with the top dome made of glass for the best view of the city.

"Tomorrow, we'll stop by there so you can see the city." She pointed to the building. With the sun setting, the view was gorgeous.

They joined the others and ate a delicious meal made of locally grown fruits and vegetables, as well as farm-raised meats. As they left, they were able to catch Keely's attention.

"Well, hello, Captain. I hope you enjoyed the meal?"

"It was wonderful. I have a favor to ask of you."

"What can I help you with, Captain?"

"I need a witness."

"A witness? I don't understand."

"We're getting married tomorrow," Torin said.

Keely's eyes widened. "Oh! Congratulations! Tremol and I had our ceremony on the Concordance just before we left Earth. I would be honored to be your witness." Keely gave her a big hug. "What time are you having the ceremony?"

"I hadn't thought that far ahead."

"If you do it after 1000 hours, we will both be free. The

meetings start at 0900 hours tomorrow. After that, we don't need to return here until 2000 hours when we load everyone up to head back to the Concordance."

"Perfect. I'll see you at 1030 hours, on the Concordance, deck 7, on the bridge."

She and Torin strolled along the sidewalks looking at the storefronts in the downtown area of the city. She spied something in one of the stores.

"Wait here."

She rushed inside and bought some items for her mating ceremony. She found two rings that would work, as well. After paying for her treasures, she met up with Torin and they headed back to the Concordance.

"So, what's in the bag?" Torin asked.

"You'll see it tomorrow at our ceremony."

"I've been thinking a lot about this and I don't regret us getting married, I mean, having this mating ceremony. I really love you, Gadara. I realized that I didn't want to lose you."

"But?"

"What would have happened to me if I didn't become your mate? If you had never asked me to be your mate, what would have happened to me?"

25

She waited until they were alone in her quarters to answer his question.

"I wanted you from the beginning, but I didn't realize it until we did laundry together. That kiss sealed it for me." She paced back and forth in her small room. Torin sat in her easy chair, waiting to hear her out.

"But when you were undergoing the procedure to remove those implants, seeing you like that, tore at my heart."

"And when we made love?"

"Yes, I wanted you then, too. Didn't you want me as well?"

"Of course I did. I didn't know what that entailed at the time, but I still wanted you."

"I asked Admiral Esrith the same question that you asked me. What would happen to you? He said if we didn't convince you to join the Vaedran Military, you would spend your life in a prison on Vestra Major."

"You didn't ask me out of pity, did you?" He stood up.

"No! I love you. I realized I couldn't live without you in my life. I didn't *want* to live without you in my life." The tears streamed down her face. She tried to wipe them away, but Torin pulled her into his arms. She wrapped her arms around him.

"When I was alone in that cell, I realized the same thing about you. I just didn't think I deserved to have someone like you in my life."

The next morning, at 1000 hours, she sent Torin to stay with Eno until the precise moment. She slipped on the dress she bought in the shop in Sentinel City. The straps were thin and the white dress with its tiny purple flowers flowed out from her waist to her knees. She wore a pair of white shoes she had. Then she wore her hair long and pulled back a tiny bit on each side in a braid that she fastened in the back with a small hairpin to keep it in place.

Just before leaving her quarters, there was a knock at the door. When she opened it, Keely and Tremol stood outside.

"Hi, Captain. I was just checking to see if you needed anything before the ceremony," Keely said.

"Oh, thank you. I don't know if I do. This is a first for me. I usually don't go to things like this. I—" She felt the tears welling up and tried blinking them away.

Keely stepped inside and gave her a hug. She hugged her back. "I don't have any friends," she whispered.

"Well, you do now. Tremol and I had our ceremony just before we left, so this is new to me as well. You can call on us any time. For anything. I brought you something." Keely set a wreath of flowers on her head. "Genesis gave this to me on my mating ceremony day, so I'm passing it on to you."

"Thank you."

"You look beautiful, Captain," Tremol said.

"I heard you made Captain as well. Congratulations, Captain Tremol."

"Thank you. Shall we go?" He ushered the two women out the door.

She grabbed her small bag with two candles and the rings inside and took Tremol's arm.

Once they got to the flight deck, she saw the admiral standing with Eno and Torin. Torin, dressed in his Air Force Unicrin, beamed when he saw her.

"Let me take that for you," Keely said as she relieved her of the bag.

Torin took her hand. "You look gorgeous," he whispered.

"I've got to agree with him, Captain," Admiral Esrith said.

He motioned for the witnesses to step forward. "Well, I see we have some familiar faces." He smiled at Eno, then Keely and Tremol.

"Congratulations to you, Captain Tremol."

"Thank you, sir." Tremol handed the admiral a leather strap.

Then he glanced at her and Torin. "Gadara and Torin, you both understand that this binds you for life?"

"Yes, sir," Torin said. He looked at her.

"Yes, sir." She kept her eyes focused on Torin's face.

The admiral bound their wrists with the leather strap and recited a passage from the book he held. "The leather cord signifies the trials you will face together in your new life."

Eno stepped forward with a lighted candle. Tremol handed Torin one of the small candles she bought and Keely handed her the other one.

"The candle signifies the faith and hope you must have to get through these trials. Light your candles."

Both she and Torin lit their candles from the one Eno

held. Then Tremol handed a ring to Torin, while Keely handed one to her.

"Now place the ring on your mate's finger," the admiral spoke to Torin.

Torin handed his candle to Tremol and took Gadara's hand. He went to put the ring on the wrong finger, but Tremol whispered in his ear and he slipped it on her middle finger. Then it was her turn. She handed her candle to Keely and slipped the ring on Torin's middle finger. Both rings were multicolored.

"The colors stand for longevity, health, prosperity, fertility, peace, and love. I declare you as mates before these witnesses. Live long, love well, and prosper."

She blew out her candle, while Torin blew his out. Then she kissed him sweetly on the lips, but Torin had other ideas and kissed her with more passion than she expected. She heard loud cheers in the background. When she pulled away, the techs and guards who were on deck 7 clapped and cheered.

Keely patted her on the back and she saw the admiral whisper something to Eno. "Since it is late morning, we have a little surprise for you in the meeting room on deck 1. Captain Tremol and Keely will escort you there. I'll be there shortly."

"What is going on?" she asked.

"Just go with it, baby." Torin kissed her cheek.

They took the people mover up to deck 1.

"How long do we keep this binding on?" he asked.

"We removed ours as soon as we were alone." Tremol said.

Torin grasped her hand that had the leather wrapped around it and just held on.

"I like this," she said, raising their hands.

When they got off the people mover, Tremol pressed the door buzzer on the meeting room. When they stepped inside, all her new pilots and some of the older ones she had trained yelled, "Surprise!"

She tried to hide the tears, but they poured from her eyes. Torin pulled a handkerchief from his pocket. "Here, baby."

She dabbed at her eyes. "Thank you! I'm touched."

"Yay, Captain Gadara!" someone yelled. Then there were cheers and clapping.

She laughed. Then she noticed there was food set out on the table. "What are you waiting for? Let's eat!"

Someone handed her and Torin a drink and Torin made a toast. "To the best pilot I've ever met." And he touched his glass to hers, then took a sip. Everyone else raised their glasses and said, "To Captain Gadara."

26

After a couple hours of partying and drinking, she and Torin spent the rest of the afternoon and early evening making love and enjoying each other's company. She wouldn't think about meeting with the Special Missions Team until tomorrow. Her new pilots were on their own for FTMs and she was officially done on the Concordance. Her new home would be wherever the Missions Team went.

"We'll have to get you a new wardrobe," she said when Torin went to shower that evening.

"I owe Eno for a unicrin." He dried off then hung up his towel.

"I'm going to miss this ship," she said. A sadness overtook her.

"How long have you been on this ship?" he asked while dressing in his Air Force uniform.

"Ten anos."

"Anos? Does that mean years?"

She sat up in bed. "I think so."

"Get dressed and we'll go for a walk," he said.

"Walk? Where?"

"Around the ship. Or if we are still over Vestra Major, we can go for a walk there."

She quickly showered and dressed in her officer unicrin. They walked around each deck, slowly working their way up to the Officers Lounge.

When they stepped inside, the place was packed. Keely walked toward them. "Come and join us," she said. She cut between them and wrapped her arms through theirs and brought them to her table. Tremol, Adam, Genesis and the Joint Chiefs of Staff were at one table. Tremol and Adam got up and brought a couple chairs to the table.

"Thank you," she said. Once she and Torin sat down, Keely leaned close.

"We've got to stick together," she said. She motioned in a circular pattern. "We are all newlyweds as we call it on Earth."

"That means newly mated," Torin explained.

"Oh. Well, now I feel more at home," Gadara said.

"Is the admiral here?" Torin asked. He looked around the room.

"No. He's in meetings with the Vaedran Council of Nations," General Thompson said.

"We asked for their help to defend against the greys and Draconians," Admiral Johnson added. "At this time, we have no way to defend against the threat they present."

"I thought you were going to order ships and weapons," Torin said.

"Oh, we have," General Stevens said. "But they won't be ready in time." He glanced at Adam. "You're the one who has premonitions? Do you know when they will happen?"

"No. I don't. I just see what will happen and hope to God I can get there in time to stop it."

"Can you tell where this attack is coming from?"

"Only that the alien ships are encircling the Earth and firing on it."

Torin turned to the two generals who were closest. "I know where their bases are on the moon. That's where they will launch from if we are talking about the greys."

"Why do you think that?" Admiral Halsey asked.

"The greys moved the moon into position eons ago. That's what created the great flood in the bible. It's their moon and they extract helium from it. Helium is what powers their ships.

"Are you sure?" Admiral Johnson asked.

"Positive."

Gadara touched his arm. "Torin?" She didn't like where this conversation was going. Her heart rate shot up.

He wrapped his hand over hers. "It's all right, Gadara." He winked at her.

"When were you planning on heading back to Earth?" she asked.

"We thought we would have another couple days of meetings, but with Adam's premonition, we don't know how much time we have before this happens," General Stevens said.

"I have a meeting with the Special Missions Team tomorrow," she said.

"The meetings tonight will determine when we leave to go back to Earth," Keely said.

"Is the admiral planning on making an announcement tonight?" she asked.

"That's the one thing none of us is certain about," Tremol said.

Gadara tossed and turned in her sleep. Torin wrapped her in his arms to comfort her. "It's okay, baby. I got you."

"I can't lose you, Torin. I can't." Her dreams scared her.

"I'm right here, Gadara. I'm not going anywhere." He brushed the hair from her face.

"Promise me you'll go with me to speak to the Special Missions people tomorrow."

"Sure, baby. I'll go with you."

She clung to him until she fell asleep.

The next morning, Gadara woke early and got dressed. Torin awoke while she was fixing her hair.

"Good morning, baby." He kissed her cheek while she was brushing her hair.

"Good morning." She stopped to watch him move his naked, muscular body into the cleansing compartment. She would never get tired of watching that.

Once he was dressed, they went to the eating hall

together. "This is a first for us," he said. They got their trays of food and went into the Officers eating area. Once they sat down, Torin looked through the glass that separated them from the others.

"I used to sit over there and watch you eat alone. It bothered me to see someone as beautiful as you eating by yourself."

She touched his arm. "I won't ever be alone again," she said. She still felt a sadness tugging at her, like it was the last time she would be eating here. "After today, we'll start a new life with the Special Missions group."

"Are you excited about it?" he asked.

She stopped eating and thought about how she felt. "It's not excitement, it's more like bittersweet. Leaving something I've been a part of for so long and going to something new."

"I'm excited for us. Every day will be a new adventure."

She smiled. "I like that. I think I will enjoy being a part of an adventure with you."

They finished eating and walked to deck 7 to see what time the ships would be heading out to Vestra Major.

"Good morning, Captain!" The guard saluted her.

She saluted back. "Can you tell me when the first ships will be leaving for Vestra Major?"

"The first ships are scheduled for 0900 hours, Captain, but Admiral Esrith informed us last night that things could change at any time."

She glanced at her chrono. It was only 0748 hours. "We'll be back. Thank you."

She and Torin headed back to her quarters. "We might as well pack up." She pulled out a small duffle stuffed in a drawer and packed her unicrins, extra boots and toiletries.

"Do you have anything to pack?" she asked him.

"I've got everything I own. Of course, if we were on Earth, I do have a few extra clothes besides uniforms."

There wasn't enough time to wash the bedding, but they did have time to strip the bed. She gave the room one last look and headed out the door.

Torin took her duffle from her as they headed to the flight deck. When they arrived, the pilots were milling around the bridge, waiting for their orders.

"Hello, boys," she said to the group.

"Captain!" They all stood at attention. She saluted them.

"So, who is the first one out?"

Eno stepped forward. "That would be me, Captain."

"Can we ride with you?"

"I would be honored, Captain Gadara ni Conolly." He saluted.

Torin glanced at Gadara and Eno. "Is that how it works here?"

"You have two names, so I take your last name."

"That's how we do it on Earth, except you would be Gadara Conolly," Torin said.

"Pilots, to your ships," Eno ordered everyone.

The pilots dispersed and she and Torin followed Eno to the ship he would be flying. A few moments later, the ships filled with other dignitaries and crew, making their way to Vestra Major.

The short trip was uneventful, but Torin took in the gorgeous sights from space and entering the atmosphere of Vestra Major. Now that it was daylight, he could see what he had missed the day they arrived.

The tallest building was the Sentinel Tower. It was round

with a glass, dome-shaped top so the 360-degree views were available to everyone. The trees weren't as tall as the building, but instead, set the building off with the different green hues. They landed at the depot a short distance away, where they had landed the last time he was here.

He stood up and took the duffle down from the overhead storage when Eno announced their arrival. He offered Gadara his arm and escorted her off the transporter.

"Where to, baby?"

"We need to get to the Tower. The Special Missions Team is based there."

Arm in arm, they walked toward the beautiful building. He noticed the vehicles they used were flying. There were no cars. The depot was used for transporter ships.

"Where do the smaller ships berth?"

"On top of the depot. There are several depots around the city just like this one."

Once inside the Tower, Gadara located the people movers. There was a sign next to them that listed all the offices on each floor.

"There." She pointed to the Special Missions office.

They made their way to the tenth floor. The way the building was designed, each floor had an intersection in the middle where there were windows on each end so that you still had views of the town from every direction.

Once inside the office, they were both invited to sit and wait. Some things are the same everywhere. He set the duffle down by his feet. After a few minutes, Gadara was called to the desk. She went in alone.

"Gadara ni Hovsep?" the woman at the desk asked.

"It's Gadara ni Conolly now."

"You have a mate?"

"Yes, I do." She couldn't help smile.

"When you applied to this program, you did not have a mate. You should have informed us."

"I'm informing you now. We just had our ceremony yesterday."

"We only have so many slots for mated couples. All we have is a single for you."

"Couldn't you make an exception?"

"This program is to set up colonies on other planets. The slots for couples are filled. We can put you on the next ship returning from Alpha Centauri."

"When will that be?"

"Six months to a year."

"Oh, no. That won't work."

"Well, you can always remain in the Star Force."

"How much time do I have to think about it?"

"If you want to remain on the Concordance, you have until morning to report back to Admiral Esrith. They will be leaving with the Reliance and Endeavor on a military exercise in the Earth System."

"And if I choose not to remain on the Concordance?"

"You can file your exit papers through your Comm-pad so you can retire."

She stood and left the office. Heartbroken and disappointed, she didn't see what was so special about the program before. Maybe because she was single and wanted a mate?

She found Torin waiting for her. He stood and approached her.

"What's wrong?"

"Everything about that program is wrong. I don't know what I thought I was doing when I applied. Just because we are a mated pair, there's no room for us."

"What?"

"The program was to set up colonies on other planets. All the single people would become mated pairs."

"And you applied when you were single."

"Yes."

He wrapped his arm around her. "Baby, we have options."

"My options are to remain on the Concordance or retire."

"Remember when I was being interrogated for hours the other day?"

"Yes?"

"Admiral Johnson of the Space Force asked me to consider their Mars program. They have a Secret Space Program going on there now and they plan a couple things on Mars' two moons."

"Will they have room for me?"

"I won't do it unless you're with me."

"She told me the Concordance was leaving in the morning."

"I guess we better get back then."

"Not until we get you some clothes."

After some shopping and a light meal, they caught the last transporter heading back to the Concordance. Torin stuffed Gadara's duffle and his bags of clothes into the overhead compartment.

"Hello, Conolly," Admiral Johnson said. He passed their seats, moving toward the back.

"Admiral, is that offer still good on your Mars Mission?"

"Why, yes, Conolly, it is."

"Captain Gadara and I would like to join your team."

"Splendid! Let's talk about it tonight in the Officers Lounge."

"You got it, sir."

Admiral Johnson leaned down, "You'll be glad to know the Pleiadians have agreed to join us as well, in our missions."

Gadara stood up. "What do your missions entail, Admiral?"

"We want to create colonies, of course, but we plan to make our own water source, our own oxygen, terraform the planet, grow our own food, and prepare to bring people there to live and visit."

He sat behind them and was joined by General Stevens.

"Since you both seem interested in the Space Force, do either of you have any recommendations for flight instructors to teach my people how to fly your ships?" General Stevens asked.

"I would recommend Eno ni Esrith," Gadara said.

"The admiral's son?"

"Yes, sir. He is one of my best pilots."

❧ 28 ❧

Admiral Johnson was sitting at a table in the Officers Lounge with Keely and Tremol when Conolly and Gadara entered. Johnson waved them over.

As they sat down, Keely asked Johnson a question. "Tell me, Admiral, are you getting anything out of this visit to the Vaedra System?"

"My, yes. Admiral Esrith has allowed us on the bridge to see what happens from day to day. He's even allowed us to take over at different times as well as asking our opinion on decisions he's had to make. I think it's brought the branches of our military closer together as far as coordinating attacks or use of resources. We've been strategizing on what to do about this premonition of Adam's and worse case scenarios."

"That's a good thing, isn't it?" Keely asked.

"Yes. If we make it back in time, we'll be able to coordinate our efforts in fighting the greys and the Draconians. We've been meeting with the admirals of the Reliance and the Endeavor this morning." Admiral Johnson pulled something out of his jacket and handed it to Conolly.

Gadara ordered a couple Detonators, while he looked at the card.

"I'll need you and Captain Gadara to fill out forms on this website so I can get you both on the payroll." Johnson pointed to the web address on the back of the card.

"How will that work sir, since I'm officially dead?"

"I'll get you a new ID when we return. We'll be doing things a little differently than the Black Government operates."

Admiral Esrith entered with Eno, General Stevens, General Thompson, and Admiral Halsey. Keely and Tremol grabbed some extra chairs, while he and Gadara moved some tables into place.

The barkeep brought the two Detonators. "Looks like I'm going to have to order more tables and chairs for this lounge, Admiral," the barkeep said.

"Ah, I see you changed your mind about the Special Missions Team, Captain Gadara?" Esrith glanced at Gadara.

"It's not what I thought it would be, sir. And they didn't have room for both of us."

"Well, it's their loss. So what have you decided?" Esrith asked.

"You could say we're going with a better option," Conolly said.

"Can we travel with you to Earth, Admiral?" Gadara asked.

"Of course. Your quarters are still yours, Captain, for as long as you need them."

"I hope you won't mind us borrowing Eno for a while to teach our Air Force pilots how to fly your ships?" General Stevens asked.

"Eno?" the admiral asked.

"It's a temporary assignment, Admiral. After our military exercises on Earth," Eno said.

"He came highly recommended. We plan to combine our pilots so he can cover the Air Force, Navy, and Space Force." Admiral Halsey said.

"And what about the Army? We have pilots as well, you know," General Thompson said.

"Well, in that case, we'll have to give him a raise," Halsey said.

"We have a lot of work ahead of us." Thompson said.

"How did your talks with the Pleiadians go?" Admiral Esrith asked.

"They are sending leaders for each of our branches to work with us in restructuring our militaries to be space-capable in all aspects. We have to re-think everything from a different perspective now," Johnson said.

"Yes, and they said there is a way to detect whether or not the Draconians are embedded in our military," Halsey said.

"Good. That's another battle altogether. Did you get a date when your ships will be ready?" Esrith asked.

"The battleships will be ready in a couple months." Johnson said.

"Yes, and the Pleiadians are traveling on the Reliance," Halsey said.

"The Pleiadians have had extensive experience with the Draconians and their Dark Fleet. I've been doing research on them. I suggest you gentlemen do the same on the Comm-Pads I lent you earlier. You may come up with something we hadn't thought of yet," Esrith said.

"What time will we be leaving?" General Thompson asked.

"0600 hours. We are awaiting supplies. Once everything is on board, we will leave."

"I guess we should do a head count of all our dignitaries," Keely said.

"I agree." Tremol stood and escorted Keely out the door.

"I just realized we need to do some laundry," Gadara said.

"Oh, yes." Conolly stood as he remembered their bed was stripped earlier and never remade. "Good night everyone," he said as he escorted Gadara to their quarters.

$\maltese$ 29 $\maltese$

Six days later, above the Earth's atmosphere, a network of space ships could be seen across the United States, pounding the country with bursts of energy, shutting down the power grids, communications, air and vehicle traffic everywhere. Then the network of space ships moved across the Atlantic and hammered Europe the same way.

"Pilots, to your ships!" Admiral Esrith ordered. "Wing ships, take out the ships targeting the planet."

A wave of ships left the Concordance. A second wave left the Reliance, and a third wave came from the Endeavor.

Torin and Gadara watched from the bridge, along with Keely and Tremol, Adam and Genesis.

"Let's go kick some Draconian ass," Torin said. He grabbed Gadara's hand and headed for deck 7.

Keely stood watch, holding onto Tremol's hand. "I can't believe they're attacking my Earth like that."

Tremol's Comm unit went off. "Kim to Security Command."

"Security Command, go ahead."

"Something's happening to the Earthen prisoner. He's convulsing, sir."

"I'm sending Yao to help you."

Keely noticed the skies lighting up in a fire fight. The space ships were fighting back.

"Wedge ship pilots, assist the wing ships," Admiral Esrith called out.

Another wave of ships left the Concordance, then from the Reliance, and from the Endeavor.

"Yao to Security Command!"

"Go ahead, Yao."

"Kim is dead, sir. And the prisoner has escaped."

"Tremol, that's our prisoner." Keely said. She and Tremol headed to the brig. Right behind them were Genesis and Adam.

"How the Vaedran hell did he escape?" Tremol said.

Tremol looked at the lock on the empty cell. "He must have gotten the yav from Kim," Tremol said.

Genesis was attending Kim. "His throat has been cut." Adam held Kim's head while Genesis prayed over him.

Keely examined the inside of the cell. "What is this slime on the floor?" She scraped it up onto the card she found not far from the cage door. "Let's see if Conn can tell us what this is."

"That's some nasty stuff," Tremol said.

They hurried to the Med Facilities on deck 4. Conn put the slime under her microscope.

She uttered some foreign words. "Where did you find this?"

"In the cell where the prisoner escaped."

"This is not human." She repeated the strange words while flipping through some charts near the microscope.

"This is Draconian!"

"What?"

"This is Draconian. We have a Draconian on board the ship!"

Tremol's Comm unit came on again.

"Pressurize deck 7. Now!"

Tremol grabbed her hand and they ran to the flight deck.

"Security Command, this is Yao. I need help on deck 7."

Several guards arrived at the same time as Tremol and Keely.

"Captain! Are you all right?" Keely assisted the guard in bringing Gadara into the pressurized area.

"What happened?"

"Torin! Where is Torin? Someone stunned me from behind. Torin and I were heading out in the wedge ship."

"I found her unconscious near where the wedge ship was before takeoff. It left and I saw her on the ground," Yao said.

"Did anyone get a read on the last ship that left?" Tremol called on his Comm unit?

"There were two life forms on the last ship," a system tech reported back.

"Do you think that was Porter on that ship?" Keely asked.

"Porter or something else," Tremol said.

Several people walked past with a hover gurney and a covered body.

"I couldn't save Kim," Genesis said. She and Adam joined them on the bridge of deck 7. Adam had his arm around Genesis. Her hands were bloody.

"Tremol, I need your help." Gadara put on her helmet and headed for the transporter below.

Keely pulled him into a kiss. "Come back safe."

"I love you, Keely."

Tremol grabbed a helmet and left with Gadara. Keely,

Genesis and Adam watched from the bridge of deck 7 as the two headed out in a transporter.

"Torin said he knew where the bases were," Gadara said, doing the pre-flight as quickly as she could.

"On Earth?"

"No, on the moon."

She put in the destination and they were off toward the moon. She picked up a blip of his ship in the distance. She shoved the transporter into high gear.

"I hope we're not too late."

"Where are we going?" Torin asked.

"To the dark side of the moon."

"You're not going to get away with this."

"Oh, but I am. Your Earth is already under attack. It will be a matter of time now before she falls to us."

Torin flew low across the moon, drawing fire from their hidden weapons.

"Pull up," Porter shouted.

Torin kept low, firing back as he went.

"Stop firing!"

He came across the first set of buildings and pulled up enough to skim the surface.

"You're too low, pull up!"

Torin fired again and Porter slammed his fist into Torin's face.

"Do that again and I'll crash this ship," he said.

"Then you'll kill both of us."

"Yeah, but no one will mourn your death, lizard man."

Porter punched Torin again, and Torin yawed hard left, crashing Porter into the building in front of them as he reached for his helmet.

. . .

Gadara saw the explosion and fire. "No!"

"Take the controls," she shouted as she unhooked her harness. Tremol pulled up over the downed craft while it burned.

Gadara opened the escape hatch in the floor as Tremol set the transporter over the overhead seal on the wedge. She tapped on the oxygen in her helmet and climbed through the opening between the ships. Flames and smoke greeted her as she dropped down behind the pilot seats.

Torin was slumped over, sitting next to a mangled lizard-looking creature.

Thank God he had his helmet on. She checked for the oxygen level. She worked quickly to unhook his harness, and was able to pull him out without much effort, thanks to the low gravity. She guided his limp body through the opening, shoved him to the side, and quickly locked the floor in place.

"We're being shot at!" Tremol shouted. They couldn't return fire in this position.

"Get us out of here!" she said.

Once the pressurization was stable, she pulled off Torin's helmet to check his vitals. His beautiful face was bloody and bruised but he had a strong pulse. "He's alive!"

A couple shots sizzled past the ship and then another explosion. This time, the Concordance fired back at the moon base, blowing up the weapons cache that was used against them.

Gadara felt along Torin's arms for anything broken and found a laser wound on his arm. "We'll have to get him to Conn or Genesis for healing," she said.

They headed to the Concordance, while some wedge ships did flybys, firing on other locations that had shot back.

Once Torin was safe, she joined Tremol at the Nav-U-Comm. "We missed one," she said. She fired on a small hill that fired up at the Concordance. "Got it!" She enjoyed watching the small explosion that erupted. "That's for Torin Conolly!"

~

Once inside the Concordance, Gadara called on her Comm unit. "I need help from a healer right away."

Another hover gurney was brought to the transporter and Torin was placed on it. They got him to the bridge and Conn worked on him until they were at the Med Facilities.

Genesis and Adam arrived. Gadara held Torin's hand while Conn prayed over him. Finally, Conn did a scan over him to see if there was anything else going on.

"Nothing appears broken, but he will need time to recover."

❦ 30 ❦

orin slept a long time. Gadara remained at his side, holding his hand and praying for a miracle.

Genesis stopped by and massaged her shoulders. "Any response yet?"

"No. I'm worried about him."

"Whenever there is a head injury, you have a long sleep time," Genesis said.

Adam walked up with Tremol and Keely. "We brought you something to eat."

"Oh, thank you." *That was kind of them.* "I really need to use the cleansing compartment, but I don't want to leave him."

"We'll stand watch for you, if you'd like?" Genesis said.

She glanced at each concerned face. Grateful for their help. She realized this was her best chance to go.

"I'll go with you," Keely said.

Confused at Keely's offer, she wanted to refuse her company. "I can find it myself," she said.

Keely wrapped her arm around Gadara. "This is what women on Earth do. We support one another."

As the two of them walked out of the Med Facilities, exhaustion overtook her and tears streamed down her face. Keely was quick to hand her a tissue.

"I don't know what I'd do without him," she said.

Keely patted her back. "You're a strong woman, Captain. But I think everything will be fine. From what Genesis told me about healing, Torin's recovery is normal."

She splashed water on her face. Keely handed her a towel, then patted her back.

"If you ever need someone to talk to, I'm here for you. I know how hard it is to find a good man. Tremol and I have only been together twelve days now and I know I'll be learning new things about him for a long time to come."

"Thank you. I've never had any real friends before," she said.

"I would feel honored to have you as my friend," Keely said.

She turned and gave Keely a hug. "The feeling is mutual."

When they returned to the Med Facilities, Conn was there. Gadara sat next to Torin again and picked up his hand, rubbing it.

"His vitals are good. We must wait until he is ready to rejoin us," Conn said.

She felt him squeeze her hand. She stood up and gazed at his face.

"What is it?" Conn asked.

Torin took a deep breath and opened his eyes. "Ah, I love looking at your face when I wake up," he said.

She bent and kissed him. He kissed her back, reaching up and touching her face. Her heart rate shot up when she heard cheering behind her.

"What's going on?" He glanced around the room and realized he was not alone.

"You've been asleep for over fifteen hours," Tremol said.

He sat up and rubbed his face. Then he glanced at each person in the room. "Porter's a damn reptile."

"What do you remember?" Gadara asked him.

He thought for a moment. "I remember getting into the wedge ship, looking over at you and seeing that hideous lizard face."

"Your face was all bruised," she said. She caressed his cheek.

Torin touched her hand. "I made the mistake of asking where you were. I didn't know he had fast reflexes." Torin kissed her hand. "What's happened since then?"

"You crashed your ship. I thought I taught you better landing skills than that," she teased.

"Oh, I did that on purpose. He wanted me to land inside their command base so they could reverse engineer the ship. So, I crashed his side of the ship into the building just before the command building."

"The Concordance took out that base after we rescued you," she said.

He swung his legs over the side of the bed. "Am I clear to go, Conn?"

"How do you feel?"

"Like I could kick some Draconian ass," he said.

"You're too late," Tremol said.

"What did I miss?"

"Well, after the Concordance took out that base, nothing will be leaving the moon. The Concordance will see to that."

"Good. What about Earth?" Torin asked.

"The Reliance and Endeavor are covering Earth. There were

no casualties on our side, but we're not sure about theirs. We've got some of our pilots and your military checking on the downed ships. We're waiting word from them now," Tremol said.

"It could take a while since they had a network of ships flying over the planet. We went ahead of our dignitaries to see if it was safe to return them. They are in lockdown now at the White House for debriefing and then they will be released. I think the Joint Chiefs of Staff will be quite busy for some time," Keely said.

"If the Draconians can change shape, how are we going to know if they're embedded in our military?" Torin asked.

"There's a simple test. I have the scientists perfecting it now so we can administer it and see the results immediately," Conn said.

"What kind of test?" Adam asked.

"A blood test. We administered it to the dignitaries after Keely discovered the discharge in the cell. We wanted to make sure we had no other surprises on board before releasing them back to Earth. We sent one of our Med techs, along with a guard, to administer the test to the President's Council members." Conn said.

"Why a guard?" Torin asked.

"If they refuse the test, they are most likely a Draconian. In which case, the guard can stun them temporarily and administer the test while they are unconscious."

"And if they are Draconian?" Adam asked.

"They will lock them up until they decide what to do with them," Conn said. "Now, we are making tests as fast as we can so more can be tested. This will be a first step to eliminating the Draconian threat."

Torin stood and stretched. "Any chance of getting a meal?"

"Here." Gadara picked up the food container her new

friends had brought for her. "We'll share this. We've got a couple hours before the mid-day meal, so this will have to do."

She and Torin headed to her quarters.

"Any news from Admiral Johnson?" Torin asked.

"No, but they plan another meeting with the Pleiadians on the Reliance in a couple days. We'll catch him then."

❦ 31 ❦

A couple days later, Admiral Johnson sent word to the Concordance for her and Torin to meet him on the Reliance.

"We have a lot of work ahead of us," Admiral Johnson said. He handed Torin some credentials.

She watched Torin look over the cards. "Torren Conley?"

"It's a new ID. What do you think?"

"Well, it's technically the same, just a different spelling."

"Different Social Security and address, too."

"Edwards Air Force Base?"

"With the disclosure of the Black Government, the President exposed a lot of information about the UFOs to the general public," Johnson continued. "More information came out from some former employees, so now there are several investigations going on simultaneously. The bottom line is we already have a colony on Mars, living underground."

"We do?" Torin asked.

"Yes, but something is happening on her moons, which we will investigate ourselves. In the meantime, Admiral Esrith is loaning us your wing ship, Captain, so you two can get to Edwards Air Force Base for training. By the time you finish your training, our ships should be ready."

"This is it, baby." Torin took her hands in his. "A new life for both of us."

"I can't wait. This will be our first adventure together," she said.

"Technically, our first adventure was you rescuing my ass from a Draconian lizard man."

END

BATTLE FOR EARTH

COMING SOON

CHAPTER ONE

The White House

"Mr. President, I'm Chief Medical Officer Conn from the Concordance, and these are my counterparts, CMO Shim from the Reliance and CMO Torres from the Endeavor." She shook the outstretched hand of the President, and watched as the others did the same.

"We are also healers," she said.

"Have a seat," the President said. He gestured to the chairs in the room.

She bowed and sat down. "The three of us have been working in our labs, creating the blood test that will show you who is human and who is not."

"We have blood tests here as well," the President said.

"Yes, but I assure you, this test will let you know immediately so you can take swift action."

"What do you mean by that?"

"The Draconians won't stand still for this. They will fight or run. If they refuse the test, we have our security forces who will stun them temporarily so they can be tested. If they are not human, you must decide whether to destroy them or hold them prisoners."

"Do you think it's that serious?" the President asked.

"Yes, sir. It is," CMO Torres said. "The Draconians embed themselves into government agencies where they take over that government."

"They gain control of planets from within," Conn said.

"Have you had recent turmoil and violence in your part of your world?" CMO Shim asked.

"Yes, actually. It's been happening all over the planet, especially after UFO sightings," the President said.

"UFO sightings?" Conn asked.

"Unidentified flying objects," the President said.

"It is worse than I thought," Conn said. She glanced at her counterparts.

"Do you have labs that can duplicate our blood tests?" CMO Torres asked.

"Yes, we do."

"We need to test everyone at the lab first to avoid sabotage. We also need to test everyone in your government," Conn said.

"Everyone?"

"Yes, sir. Otherwise, you won't know whom to trust," CMO Torres said.

The Concordance, Above Earth's Moon

Adam Davis paced back and forth in the small quarters he shared with his mate. "Genesis, I can't stand by and do nothing." He ran a hand through his hair. "That's my planet. My home."

"And my home is with you," she said. She stood and touched his arm.

He stopped pacing.

"Whatever you decide, I am with you."

"Let's go find Tremol and see what we can do," he said. He put his arm around her and headed to the people mover.

Captain Tremol and his mate, Keely, sat across from Captain Gadara and her mate, Torren Conley, in the Officers Lounge on deck 1.

Keely waved them over. Adam sat next to Torren and Genesis sat next to Keely.

"When do you start your new assignment?" Keely asked Captain Gadara.

"We start tomorrow," she said. She touched Torren's thigh and squeezed.

He smiled at her before speaking. "They are sending us to Edwards Air Force Base." He glanced at Keely and Captain Tremol.

"Edwards? Isn't that where they keep alien ships?" Keely asked.

"Yes. We will be training for two months before they send us to the moons of Mars," Gadara said. She smiled at Torren. He winked at her.

"What about you two?" Keely glanced at him and Genesis.

"That's why we are here," Genesis said.

The barkeep brought some drinks for Tremol, Keely, Gadara, and Torren. "What are you two having?"

"Two ales, please," Adam said.

When the barkeep left, Adam glanced at Tremol. "What's the word on Earth?"

"Conn and the Chief Medical Officers from the Reliance and Endeavor left with their assistants and security for the White House," Tremol said.

"They are initiating the testing," Keely added. "We were told to wait here for further instructions."

"What about all the dignitaries?" Adam asked.

"After they were all tested here, Keely and I flew them to the White House with our security. They are in a bunker, on lockdown, until the building is cleared of all Draconians," Tremol said.

"Genesis and I want to help. What can we do?" he asked.

The barkeep returned with his drinks. Before leaving, he glanced at the entrance. Everyone turned to see Admiral Esrith walk in with Eno and a couple other people.

"We just got word from the Reliance that their scientists have created a mist that will penetrate the skin of non-humans and expose who they really are. It's much quicker than the blood tests." The admiral, Eno, and the two others stood beside their table.

"Something tells me there's bad news with this," Adam said.

"You're right, Adam. The word from the Endeavor is the damn reptiles have taken over the White House."

FOR MY READERS

September, 1989, I drove home from a Campfire outing, where I was the Campfire leader, along with a parent and seven children. Three of the children were mine and two belonged to the parent. The other two children were siblings.

We had spent the afternoon hiking along trails at Ft. Pickens in Gulf Islands National Seashore, in Florida. We played along the beach, walked through the fort and then headed home.

My Chevy Van was customized where there were two seats up front, a long seat behind the driver's seat, and a bed behind that. Five of the children sat on the bed, chatting as kids do (ages 5-7). My youngest sat up front in his car seat, beside me, while the parent and his younger daughter sat behind me. My air conditioning wasn't working, so the windows were down as I drove down the deserted beach road, in the dark. It was maybe 7pm or so. On either side of the road were sugar white sand dunes which glowed in the moonlight, but tonight, the moon was hidden by clouds.

On my right, was the Gulf of Mexico. Something dark rose up from the sand, in the air. Then, in seconds, it was on my left about 25 ft above me and maybe 10 ft out in front of my car, pacing me for more than 7 miles. It was circular and had 'chasing' lights that went in a circle below it. I think they were red and yellow, I don't remember now, but there were two colors. Before I studied this thing, I made a comment to the parent about the Navy doing helicopter maneuvers on the beach (which I had seen in daylight hours years before).

He said, "I design helicopters for the Navy and that's no helicopter I've ever seen." That comment sent goosebumps all over me. Then I realized there was no sound and I was looking at a UFO.

During that period of time, several sightings occurred in the Gulf Breeze and Pensacola, Florida areas. The military bases that surrounded us denied that it was them.

This incident had an impact on me over the years, compelling me to write my first book, "The Abduction." Although that's the only thing I remember about that day, it has propelled me to write other sci-fi stories from a 'what if?' scenario. Since then, I have read a lot of conspiracy theories and come to the decision that some of these are actual facts the government has been deliberately drip feeding us over the years.

I write because I have to. This incident got me started. Once I finished the first story, the secondary characters started telling me their stories and The Vaedra Chronicles were born. The next book, "Battle for Earth," is the end of the first segment of The Vaedra Chronicles I call The Genesis Tales. There will be more.

***

**As promised in a blog post, here is the recipe for the Deto-
nator. As a former mixologist, this is a recipe I created (and
tested), so it's all good. Hope you enjoy it. **

Remember, never drink and fly (or drive)

ABOUT THE AUTHOR

Ester López is a writer and publisher and lives in the Smoky Mountains, where she has been writing sci-fi and paranormal adventure romances for almost 30 years.
To keep up to date on Ester's book releases and book signings, please join her Readers Group at:
www.esterlopez.com

Follow Ester's Blogs at:
www.esterlopez.com
www.AuthorBlogSpot.esterlopez.com

To purchase Ester's books, go to her publisher's website at:
www.writingphotographicservicesllc.com

ALSO BY ESTER LÓPEZ

The Vaedra Chronicles

Book 1 The Abduction

Book 2 Revenge

Book 3 Betrayed

The Angel Chronicles

Book 1 The Quest

Book 2 Between Heaven and Earth

Children's Books

The Adventures of Charlie and Ellie